You're So Sweet

You're So Sweet

BALLET SCHOOL CONFIDENTIAL

CHARIS MARSH

Editor: Shannon Whibbs
Design: Jennifer Scott
Printer: Webcom

Library and Archives Canada Cataloguing in Publication

Marsh, Charis
You're so sweet / Charis Marsh.

(Ballet school confidential)
Issued also in electronic formats.
ISBN 978-1-4597-0417-6

I. Title. II. Series: Marsh, Charis. Ballet school confidential.

PS8626.A7665Y68 2012 jC813'.6 C2012-900141-4

1 2 3 4 5 16 15 14 13 12

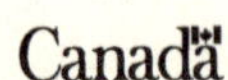

We acknowledge the support of the **Canada Council for the Arts** and the **Ontario Arts Council** for our publishing program. We also acknowledge the financial support of the **Government of Canada** through the **Canada Book Fund** and **Livres Canada Books**, and the **Government of Ontario** through the **Ontario Book Publishing Tax Credit** and the **Ontario Media Development Corporation**.

Care has been taken to trace the ownership of copyright material used in this book. The author and the publisher welcome any information enabling them to rectify any references or credits in subsequent editions.

J. Kirk Howard, President

Printed and bound in Canada.

Visit us at
Dundurn.com
Definingcanada.ca
@dundurnpress
Facebook.com/dundurnpress

Dundurn
3 Church Street, Suite 500
Toronto, Ontario, Canada
M5E 1M2

Gazelle Book Services Limited
White Cross Mills
High Town, Lancaster, England
LA1 4XS

Dundurn
2250 Military Road
Tonawanda, NY
U.S.A. 14150

This book is for ...

My mother, who reads everything I write, and
my father, who intends to.

My brothers, who thought I should have given
the dancers superpowers
or at the very least killed one of them off.

My sister, who always tells me that I am sweet.

Adrian, who thought it would have been cooler if
I had written You're So Sweet
in a journal with a fountain pen instead of
typing it on a laptop.

My grandparents, who are simply awesome.

Dundurn, because they published me, and that
was pretty cool of them.

You, because you picked my book up!

Chapter One

Julian Reese

Going back to Van today — hopefully.

Julian Reese stood at the doorway of his father's bedroom, staring at the back of his father's head. There were only three rooms in this house: the living room, which was also the kitchen and contained the couch Julian had been sleeping on all Christmas break; the bathroom; and the bedroom. Julian waited patiently for his father to answer him, propping himself up against the the door. Beside him, his backpack and small suitcase were ready and waiting. If only he could get Will off the computer, he would be on his way back to dance. There were two things in Julian's life that he was sure of at the moment. One, that dance was currently the most important thing in his life. Two, that the more firmly he was convinced of this, the more his mind wandered off on to other subjects and problems that were not helpful to think about because there was nothing he could do to fix them.

Problem one would be Julian's father.

"Will?"

Will didn't look up, his headphones plugged into his laptop, bopping in time to the music as he worked on his blog post; a marvellous work concerning Will's personal philosophy on life, as described by *William O. Reese*. Julian sighed and stepped into the room, waving his hand in front of his father's face, blocking his view of the computer.

"What?" Will turned to Julian, pulling one earphone out.

"You said you would drive me to the ferry, remember?"

"Yes, but … hey, dude, do you think you could ask Daisy if she'd take you? It's just, I'm really in the zone here."

"Daisy's working at the farmer's market," Julian explained. "It's Sunday, *remember?*" It felt like he used that word constantly where Will was concerned.

"Oh, yeah …"

River came in and wrapped his arms around Julian's legs. "Are you leaving, Jules?"

"Yeah." Julian looked down at his little brother. River had been playing in the garden and had managed to get dirt over most of his body, streaking parts of his blond curls. "I have to go back to dance, remember?"

"Why can't you dance here?"

"Because I can't, little guy. Now shush for a sec, all right? Will, I really need to go now. Like, *now.* And can you please get some food while we're out? River needs to eat, and there's nothing in the house."

Will frowned, looking around. "Oh. For sure, we should do that. Okay, let's go, you guys tell me when you're ready, and we'll go, okay?"

"We're ready," Julian assured him.

River stuck out his foot. "My shoes are already on, even." Julian looked down at River's feet. His shoes were not just on, they were also coated with mud, and there were now chunks of mud leading from the door through the living room. Julian decided to pretend not to see the mess so he didn't have to clean it up, and held out his arms to carry River into the car. He was a bit old for it at four years old, but he still liked it.

Julian walked quickly onto the ferry to Vancouver, a scowl on his face instead of his usual serene smile. He had nearly not made it, thanks to Will. He hurried through the lounges, trying to find a seat. Each bench he passed was full of loud passengers, making their way home after the holidays. Julian gave up and sat down on the floor, stretching out his long legs, and pretending he didn't see the annoyed looks of the passengers who had to get by him. His iPod wasn't loud enough to drown out the noises of the cranky people around him, and so he flipped restlessly through his songs, not able to concentrate as his brain buzzed with everything he was worried about.

A year ago Julian wouldn't have minded his dad's carefree attitude toward time, River, or in fact, toward Julian himself, but a year was a long time. Lately it seemed like every time Julian talked to his father he felt like yelling at him. Why couldn't Will see when things needed to be done? Why did Julian always have to remind him that River should be enrolled in school, that he needed to pay rent, that he wasn't allowed to drive with an expired licence?

Not to mention Problem two. Problem two was how he wasn't doing well enough at dance. He had caught enough glances and heard enough snide remarks before Christmas to know "They" thought he wasn't working hard enough. Well, he would show them what Julian Reese was capable of. He had to if he wanted to be a dancer; if he couldn't even be the best at the academy, how was he going to get a job?

Julian's phone vibrated with a text from Taylor, aka Problem three. Julian opened Taylor's text.

> Hey, u catch the 5?
> No, I'm on the 7.
> K. See u at 830-ish.

That was the problem with Taylor. He was grateful that she was going to pick him up (or her mom was), and everything, but ... *I'm a jerk,* Julian decided. *So what if Taylor is a little annoying? She tries hard to be a good friend.* It was just that Taylor tried too hard, and it was hard not to just tell her to go away sometimes. Julian could smell the fries from the cafeteria, and his stomach rumbled. He wanted to get some, but the line was sooo long ...

He wandered up to the top deck, lost in thought. He was sure that Will had been better when he was young, but the way Will was with River ... *well, carefree isn't the right word. Lazy? Maybe it's because River looks more like*

Daisy than Will. It wasn't like Daisy was an "involved" mother, either. The only thing Julian had seen her do for River all Christmas break was when they'd gone to Daisy's parents' place for Christmas dinner and she'd scraped all the turkey off his plate. Julian shook his head, remembering. *It's all right to raise the kid vegan, but most of the time Daisy forgets to feed him, period.* Julian glared at the ocean, watching as the rain beat down on the black waves and ferry deck. *I am* so *glad Taylor is picking me up*. It was already dark, and the weather seemed to be getting worse.

Finally the ferry arrived at Horseshoe Bay. Julian half ran down the walkway, weaving expertly through the tired passengers. Grabbing his suitcase from the luggage carousal, he went outside, anxiously scanning the crowd for Taylor and Charlize.

"Jules, Jules, over here!" Taylor called, waving excitedly. She was wearing a red dress coat that would have made her stand out in the middle of the Metrotown mall on Boxing Day, and she was carrying the brightest yellow umbrella Julian had ever seen. He was not surprised to see that it also had a duck at the end of the handle.

He walked over, grinning with relief that they had remembered to pick him up. "Hey, Taylor!"

"I missed you! I'm so, so excited for classes again, aren't you? Did you have fun with your family? How is River? They must've missed you, hey? Mom is, like, so stupid, she forgot how to get to Horseshoe Bay, and so we were, like, almost late, and then you would've been waiting in the dark here for us. It's so friggin' freezing out. Mom, could you *please*, like, turn on the heat? We're completely freezing?"

Julian gratefully got into the car, sinking into the seat. "Hey, Alison," he said, smiling at Taylor's little sister. Alison grinned at him, not bothering to unplug from her iPod, and then looked back down at it.

"So, Julian, Taylor said that you two were thinking of doing a *pas* together?" Charlize asked as she made her way up the curving road through Horseshoe Bay and onto the highway into Vancouver.

"Oh, yeah."

"I was thinking, we should probably do two," Taylor said. "That way we could do a contemporary *pas* and a classical."

"Uh, that sounds good," Julian agreed, slightly unsure. "The only thing is, do these *pas de deux* — do we have to pay for them?"

"Well, you have to pay an entry fee, of course, and privates and stuff … we can see how it goes. We can, like, talk about it later, right? But it would be fun, right?"

"Yeah."

"I can't wait to learn the *pas de deux* you choreographed, Julian, the way you explained it last week I think it's going be, like, so cool."

"Yeah, I hope you like it." Julian smiled. "I think it's really sweet." He had almost finished it — he just had about thirty seconds more to choreograph at the end, and hopefully he would get a chance to finish that before Taylor wanted to learn it. And it was basically the way he had described it to her on the phone: at least, it was set to the same music and had lots of lifts. He hoped that she liked it; he didn't want to have to change it if she didn't.

Mr. Yu's house was completely dark by the time they arrived. "Thanks for the ride," Julian mumbled, tired. He climbed out of the car and made his way slowly to the house, opening the front door with the minimum of noise. *Yes* ... He opened the front door as quietly as he could, walking softly in his sock feet to his room, closing the door behind him. He set his suitcase and backpack in the corner of the room, and flung himself on his bed with a sigh of relief. It was good to be back; he couldn't wait to take class tomorrow. It had been a whole two weeks without dance, and he was going through withdrawal. He set his alarm and fell asleep without unpacking.

Julian lay on his bed, staring at his cellphone as he waited for it to go off. He always woke up early when he was excited. It began to beep, and he got up, leaving his warm covers behind in a sudden rush, and scrambling into his clothes as fast as he could. It was hard to do up his jeans; he'd grown again. His sweatshirt was a bit too short in the arms and body again, too.

There were President's Choice cornflakes and milk, or Wonder Bread. Julian grimaced, but grabbed a few handfuls of cornflakes and stuffed them in a Ziploc bag to eat on the way. He wanted to get out of the house before everyone else woke up; he still wasn't used to living with people who weren't his family, and besides, he was too excited to start his day to stay inside. He grabbed his backpack and the lunch Mrs. Yu had left him in the fridge. He stepped out of the house and locked the door behind him, running down the slippery steps and out the white iron gate guarded by two white stone lions. He grinned at them and did a quick *pirouette* on the sidewalk and waltz. It was good to be back in Vancouver. He set his longboard down and began to skate to the bus stop.

As Julian reached Cambie Street, he had to stop to wait for the flood of people getting off the Canada Line to pass. He wasn't used to skating in Vancouver yet, with all the vehicles and people. At home, the only traffic was the rush down the hill to catch the ferry. Bored, Julian texted Taylor as he waited. A second later, his phone began to vibrate, and he answered it without looking at the caller ID. Taylor was the only person he knew who would call him back at six in the morning. "Hey, 'sup, Taylor?"

"Dude, did you know you sent me a text just now?"

"Yeah, sorry."

"It's okay. Hey, I forgot to ask you, are you doing Spring Seminar this year?"

"Yeah. You?"

"Yeah, I always do it. Hey ..."

Julian moved his longboard back and forth with his foot as he waited for Taylor to finish. If he didn't get going soon he would have to take the bus to get to school on time, and that would really suck.

"I was wondering, my mother was thinking of taking in a homestay. Do you think you would want to stay with us?

Julian's brain hadn't woken up enough yet to diplomatically deal with this question. "What? With you guys?"

"Yes."

"Um, I don't know, I kind of like staying with the Yus ..."

"Whatever, it doesn't really matter. So I'll see you at school?"

"K, see you." Taylor hung up and Julian stuffed his phone in his pocket as he began to whiz west down 49th Street, passing the Main Street sari shops and the East Indian restaurant on the corner. The construction companies were still working on the roads, and he weaved to avoid extraneous equipment and chunks of pavement. He grinned; ballet was making him ride his skateboard differently, he was riding with his legs turned out from the hip and his shoulders rotated back. It was raining now, hitting his cheeks, stinging as the cold wind whipped past him. He thought about Spring Seminar; he still wasn't quite sure what it was, and he was a bit nervous for it. Julian had never done it, but almost everyone else at the academy either had done it or was going to do it. Apparently guest teachers came, and there were scholarships that were handed out. The Demidovskis usually came to watch the end performance. Julian hoped that he would get a scholarship. It would be nice to prove to the Demidovskis that he was worth the full scholarship that they had given him to attend the academy.

The bus caught up to him, and Julian got on, too cold to skate the rest of the way. The morning rush had already started, and Julian tried to wedge himself in, his longboard and large backpack not helping.

"Everybody to the back, everybody to the back," the bus driver announced grumpily. "I am not leaving until everyone is *behind* the red line." Everyone shoved and muttered their way to the back. "This is the bus the students have to take to school. If you do not *need* to catch this bus at this time, you should wait until the rush is over. You are taking spots from people who need to catch this bus."

Julian eyed the baggage shelf. Depending on the bus driver, he occasionally could sit up there when it was this ridiculously busy. The bus driver saw him looking at it and shook her head. "Don't even think about it," she advised. "Hold on," she called to the back, and they lurched on their way, leaving the unlucky waiting for the next bus.

As Julian fought his way out of the bus, he laughed — Alexandra was attempting to get off the same bus, but through the back doors. "Sorry, oh sorry … God, I'm really … sorry, thanks."

"Hey Lexi, 'sup?" Julian asked, trying not to laugh.

"Geez, Jules! I didn't see you!" Alexandra started, trying to do her pack back up. "Hey, could you hold this for a sec?" She shoved a binder, some random papers, and a textbook back at him.

"Why do you have so much stuff? It's the first day back," Julian asked, holding her stuff precariously.

Alexandra managed to shove everything back inside her backpack and was just able to do up her zipper again. She held her arms out for her stuff, and Julian obediently began to fill her arms up again. "I have to bring all my locker stuff back."

"Why didn't you just leave it all there during break?" Julian asked as they walked up to the school, avoiding the massive puddles.

"I needed it," she explained. "I was working on my solos for competition, plus I meant to try and study, and finish my online chemistry course up over the break."

"Seriously? That's pretty hard core, studying on Christmas break."

"I *meant* to." Alexandra rolled her eyes. "*So* didn't happen, I only got halfway through. But it's the thought that counts, right?"

"Right. How come you're here so early?"

"I'm an idiot and I got up early because I was excited to go back to dance. I'm already tired, though!"

McKinley was one of the newer schools in Vancouver, and it was clean and bright-looking in the morning sunlight. It was a peachy sandstone colour of the sort that had been popular for public schools during the late 1990s and early 2000s, and the flag at the entrance proudly flew the United States flag. The school billboard announced that Hancock Secondary's Senior Prom would be held on June 6.

"I guess something's being filmed here again," Alexandra said. "That's cool."

"I like the new trees," Julian said, laughing. The film crew had obviously thought that McKinley Secondary had been lacking in the tree department, and had propped a row of fake trees on top of the grass leading up to the entrance and covered up the wooden bases with squares of turf.

"Classy," Alexandra agreed. She pushed open one of the front doors, and they entered their school, which seemed to have almost equal McKinley Secondary and Hancock Secondary symbols at the moment. The atrium was a huge empty space right now, and their shoes made loud squeaking noises as they walked across to one of the tables. Alexandra dumped her backpack on one of the tables with a sigh of relief. "Okay, that's better."

"Mmm, I can smell cinnamon buns," Julian said, sniffing. He looked in the direction of the cafeteria.

Alexandra made a face. "I love cinnamon buns," she said.

"Why don't you get one?" Julian asked.

"Why don't you?" Alexandra countered.

"No money," Julian answered.

"I'll buy you one."

"Really?"

"Yeah, sure. Here." Alexandra passed him a toonie, and Julian automatically took it.

"You sure?"

"Yeah."

"You just want me to get fat, don't you?"

"Pretty much, yeah." They both giggled, and Julian went over to get his cinnamon bun, coming back with a floppy sugar-and-cinnamon-drenched mess and a pile of napkins.

"Want a bite?" Julian asked, tearing a piece off and stuffing it in his mouth.

"Sure, thanks." Alexandra took a piece. "What's with the skateboard?"

"I missed it last semester, so I brought it back from the Island. And it's a longboard."

"It's cool."

"Thanks — so, are you doing that Spring Seminar thing?"

"Yeah."

"Tristan said you got a scholarship last year."

"Yeah." Alexandra frowned as she opened up her thermos of green tea and sniffed it. "It was for contemporary, though."

"Still, that's really cool."

"Yeah, I guess."

"Hey, want to hear something really weird?"

"Yeah."

"Taylor just asked me if I wanted to homestay with her family."

Alexandra frowned over the steam from her Thermos. "Don't do it," she advised. "They're nuts."

"So's Mr. Yu."

"He's a different kind of nuts. Trust me, you do not want to homestay with Taylor."

Julian nodded. The atrium was filling up around them, and he stood up, stretching out his backpack. "I'm going to get to class," he said. "I want to try and get a good seat. I hate being stuck in the front or in the back." Julian got up and left. Even though he had the same courses that he'd had last semester, they still felt better thanks to his break. Fresh new paper, new pens, and he had actually slept. He felt actually excited to take notes.

By the time Julian got out of school, the clear cold sky of the morning had turned grey, and cold rain had started to drum down. He made his way to the bus stop, walking on the grass to avoid the humongous ice and water puddle that was usually sidewalk. "I'm sooo wet!" he called out to the others as he neared the bus stop.

"Maybe not the best day to bring your skateboard?" Anna called back to him.

"Hey, so I heard from Aiko that the Demidovskis have finally decided what ballet we're doing for June show," Alexandra interrupted, her teeth chattering.

"You know what might help you warm up?" Delilah asked, shaking her head. "This." She fixed Alexandra's scarf so it was no longer purely decorative.

"So, what did they decide?" asked Taylor, skipping from foot to foot as she tried to stay warm. The slush was now more like snow, and was no longer melting but sticking. The wind started to pick up.

"*Coppelia*," Anna answered before Alexandra could.

"Well, I know what role I want," said Delilah positively. They waited. "Dr. Coppélius, ob-vi-ous-ly," said Delilah. They burst out laughing.

"I can so see you with that cane, poisoning poor Franz." Tristan laughed.

"I am so not even ready to *think* about June show," said Taylor. "Right now all I want to think about is YAGP."

"You're going to compete?" asked Alexandra, staring at her.

Taylor shrunk a little into her coat as everyone stared at her. "Yes. Mrs. Demidovski *said* I could," she added defensively.

"That's cool," Alexandra said expressionlessly. The others started sniggering.

"The Demidovskis were okay with *you* going?" Tristan asked, disbelieving.

Taylor blushed and muttered something unintelligible involving the words "thinking about," "Mrs. Demidovski said," and "my mother."

"I think," said Angela virtuously, "that you should only do competitions when you are really ready for them. Otherwise, what is the point? That's why *I'm* not going. But maybe next year, who knows, if I work hard enough?"

Tristan mimed doing a laborious arabesque behind Angela's back, reducing the rest to giggles.

"Where is that bus?" Alexandra went into the middle of the street to see if she could see it coming. "*Still* can't see it."

"Taylor," Julian said quietly, coming up to her while the others were distracted by trying to tell if the bus was in service or not, "is that the competition you were talking about? For me to do with you?"

Taylor nodded, looking surprised. "Of course. If you want to."

"Of course I want to," Julian said. "But … are the Demidovskis okay with me doing this competition? I mean, it's kind of a big deal, right?"

"Yeah," Taylor giggled. "I'm so excited."

"Yeah. Kind of scary," Julian agreed.

"Julian, how come you don't want to live at our house?" Taylor asked. "I think it would be fun."

"Uh —" Julian stammered. "It's not that I don't *want* to live with you guys, I just already live with Mr. Yu. I think it would hurt his feelings if I moved out."

"Oh, okay."

Julian stood in front of the schedule, trying to figure out which teachers they had for class. Okay, so obviously LPY was Mr. Yu's initials, as usual, but one of the slots just had an asterisk instead of a name. Who was it? Was that the academy staff's way of saying that they had no idea who was teaching today? "Tris, who's the asterix?"

"Obelix's best friend," said Tristan solemnly.

Julian stared at him blankly.

"You never read those comics?" Tristan exclaimed. "That sucks. But, seriously," he continued in a quieter voice, putting a hand on Julian's shoulder and steering him down the hallway and thus hopefully out of earshot of the academy office "that means Mr. Demidovski's teaching today. He always gets an asterisk, we're not sure if it is because he's terrified that the parents will realize he still teaches occasionally and will force him to teach their kids or if he's just hopelessly vain and wants to feel important."

"Awesome," said Julian. "I didn't know he even taught still."

Tristan grinned. "He teaches what he wants to teach, and who he wants to teach. I hate to say it, but he's kind of awesome." They went downstairs to get changed.

As they were stretching before class, everyone was completely buzzed about both the first day back and a class with Mr. Demidovski. There were small groups spread out over the room, stretching and gossiping, with Delilah skipping from group to group to make sure she didn't miss anything.

"Is his class hard?" Julian asked as he pushed Tristan's leg up to his head.

Tristan let his leg fall down and then collapsed to the ground. "Uh … depends? His class is sort of hard to describe. It's always random. Hey, do you think you could stretch my feet? Thanks. Er, I don't think you are strong enough to stretch them with your hands, do you think you could stand on them? Thanks … ow! No, that's good."

There was a sudden hush as Mr. Demidovski walked in. Holding a walking stick for emphasis, he paused in the doorway to survey his students. "Ah bea-u-tiful day, yes?" he asked, beaming around. There was flurry of smiling and nodding, and everyone

last group, anyway, what's this all about? Does he have to be so obvious about who he likes best? Julian accidentally hit Jonathon in the face, and, taking this as a sign, gave up on marking the exercise. Instead he slipped between the *barre* and the wall and leaned on the *barre,* pretending to study the second group's work. Julian wondered if Tristan and Kageki were on scholarship, too; he'd never asked and just assumed that they weren't. Finally the first group was done, and Julian stood at attention, ready to be called. He looked intently at Mr. Demidovski, willing the man to notice him. Instead Mr. Demidovski began correcting Anna.

"You must … use the music, feel the music," he explained. "Your arms, they must be like the butterfly, flying over the water — here, rotate." Mr. Demidovski got up to move Anna's arms in the right way, running his long thin hands over her back as he moved her muscles. "The back, here must hold, here must open — and give. You must always be giving the heart, the love to the audience. Yes, Anna, this! You must always do the work this way."

Julian attempted to look fascinated, along with the rest of the class. He giggled — Angela was leaning as far forward as possible without falling forward, her mouth hanging open and her eyes popped, as she stared at Mr. Demidovski. As soon as Mr. Demidovski finished speaking, she began to try and replicate Anna's movements while staring in the mirror. She was unsuccessful. Mr. Demidovski's eye drifted over her, and Julian distinctly saw him wince before he hurriedly turned back to his selected group.

"You — this — come here, please; Mr. Demidovski wishes to speak to you." Mr. Demidovski said, gesturing impatiently in Julian's direction. Julian's stomach gave a lurch, and he half-rose out of his slouch against the wall before he realized that Mr. Demidovski was actually talking to Taylor. He rested against the wall again, annoyed with himself, and wondering if anyone had noticed his mistake. He looked around, trying to look casual; no, they were all intently concentrated on Mr. Demidovski's words as he corrected Taylor. Julian wondered if he could get away with just sitting down since he wasn't dancing anyway. *Better not risk it.* Almost everyone else seemed to be working on Taylor's correction along with Taylor.

"... you have the beautiful body, the beautiful hair, body suit, now you must make it the beautiful dance," Mr. Demidovski was explaining as he made Taylor repeatedly *develope a la seconde.* "No hip! Mr. Demidovski said no hip, no clunk, must be very smooth like ice cream. You must listen to Mr. Demidovski."

Taylor's face was flushed with effort as she tried one more time, slowly drawing her foot up her leg and unfolding her working leg. She managed to bring her leg to its full extension without her usual hip shift, and shyly smiled in relief.

"Yes, this is the way you must work. The other way, it is cheap. That way you are maybe sold at the dollar store. Here this is maybe the Bay, Sears — you must work to be the one of a kind, an original, people pay much money for you. Understand?" Taylor nodded throughout Mr.

Demidovski's speech, and as soon as he was done she went quickly back into her position, smiling happily.

Julian looked at the clock; they were almost halfway through the class, and still only the first group had received any attention at all. Mr. Demidovski hadn't even changed groups yet, and Julian was getting cold from doing nothing after *barre* — now even if Mr. Demidovski did call on him he wouldn't be warmed up. The others were all marking it on the side, but there wasn't really enough room for Julian to work, he decided after a second's glance around. He felt — he didn't exactly know how he felt. Sad? Disappointed? *Seriously, picking Kageki over me? Kageki is good and stuff, but he's seriously short, and he doesn't have as good a body type as I do.*

"Julian!" hissed Jessica, elbowing him in the back. Julian came back to his surroundings with a start — Mr. Demidovski was frowning at him, and the whole class was staring at him. Julian smiled at Mr. Demidovski, slightly embarrassed, and quickly untangled himself from the *barre*, managing to knock over someone's water bottle in the process.

"You must pay attention during class time," said Mr. Demidovski, no longer bothering to look at Julian. "Otherwise you waste your classmates' time, you waste the teacher's time, you waste your time, and you waste your parents' time and money." Julian felt his face turn bright red.

Mr. Demidovski continued, and Julian spent the rest of the class in a miserable blur. *Why was I so stupid*?

Now I'm probably never going to get a correction from Mr. Demidovski. What if he takes away my scholarship because he thinks I'm not working hard enough? At last it was the end of first class. "What do we have for second class today?" Julian asked Tristan as the girls put on their *pointe* shoes.

"*Pas de deux* class with Mr. Yu? Like we always do on Wednesdays?" answered Tristan, grinning at him. "Dude, I swear, you are so spacey sometimes." He went off to practise his *pirouettes* and talk to Alexandra.

Julian shrugged and dropped to the floor, stretching his turn-out with his face pressed to the floor so he didn't have to look at anybody. The floor actually felt pretty good on his hot face, as long as he didn't think about all the sweat it was covered in from the Youth Company, who had just been in rehearsing their contemporary piece.

Mr. Yu came in with a huge scowl on his face, and everyone immediately went quiet. They eyed him warily. He strode to the front of the class, and stood there for a second. "Mrs. Demidovski," he announced with a heavy sigh, "would like to watch you today. So be good." He went to the side and dragged a chair from the side of the room to the front, and banged it down beside his chair. He eyed the space between the chairs for a second with his head cocked to one side, and then pushed the two chairs carefully farther apart, to the giggles of his students. Then he went and carefully escorted Mrs. Demidovski in, his face pained.

"Tallest to shortest, girls' line front, boys' line back," said Mr. Yu with impatience. "Quickly, quickly!" They assembled in seconds, already having their places memorized. "Tristan, take Anna, take Grace, take ... Alexandra."

Julian was next in height, and he tensed, hoping he got partnered with good people to make up for last class.

"Julian — take Taylor ..."

Taylor gave Julian a huge grin as she joined him, and he smiled back at her a second late as he waited for Mr. Yu to assign him more partners. But Mr. Yu just moved on to the other boys, giving them all three partners, even little Michael, and giving Tristan and Kageki each one more partner when he realized he was going to have two girls left over.

"Yay! Now we get lots of practice together." Taylor grabbed Julian's arm and led him to a clear place on the floor.

Julian looked over to where Tristan was practising a promenade in *attitude* with Anna. "Why do you think he only gave me one partner? I mean, I'm totally cool with it, but it is a little weird, right? Look at Kageki and Tristan's partners — they're barely going to get to work at all."

Taylor shrugged innocently, looking like a six-year-old as she brought her hands and shoulders up to her ears. "I don't know. Maybe he wants you to have a chance to really concentrate? Oh, shh, look at Mr. Yu now."

As Mr. Yu went through the exercise, Taylor and Julian marked it, with Taylor murmuring directions to Julian. As the class ran through the exercise a couple times without music to rehearse, Mr. Yu walked through the class, barking and hitting corrections. "Anna, hold your back. Jonathon, you laugh one more time, outta my class. Out." *Thwack.* "Keiko, hold your belly! You are some old grandmother? You have many, many children?" *Thwack.* Taylor winced and adjusted her *attitude* position. "You a dog? You have to go pee?" Mr. Yu asked her, peering into her face.

"No," Taylor squeaked, trying to hold her balance. She wiggled Julian's arm, and he looked at her, confused. Taylor fell off *pointe.*

"You are partnering," Mr. Yu lectured her. "This is not solo dance, this is *pas de deux.* If you want to leave, practise solo, let me know — I am sure there is nice studio upstairs, empty, you can practise all by yourself." Mr. Yu walked off.

"What did he mean by that?" Julian asked Taylor.

To Julian's surprise, Taylor glared at him. She looked like she was about to cry. Stepping back on *pointe,* she gave him her hand again. "When you stand too close — like this — I have to lean back and then I fall over. And when we turn, you have to move *with* me — otherwise I tilt, or can't move, or fall over. Okay?"

"Okaay," said Julian, drawing out the sound. "I've got it, I'll try — we're both learning here, okay?"

They worked on the combination in silence for a few moments. After a bit Taylor was still falling over, but she smiled at him when they finished, so he supposed she'd probably forgiven him. Having only one partner should have meant that Julian had more time not working than the other boys, but Taylor made Julian go over each exercise with her on the side until their turn, and after. By the time the class was almost over, Julian was more exhausted than he usually was from working with three partners. Finally it was the end, and after bowing to Taylor and Mr. Yu, and Mrs. Demidovski, and George, Julian grabbed his water bottle and prepared to flee.

Mr. Yu grabbed Julian by the shoulder and spun him around. "Mrs. Demidovski would like to have a talk with you," he said quietly. Julian looked apprehensively at Mrs. Demidovski's back as she exited the studio. "Not now, go get changed quickly and come up, talk in office," Mr. Yu clarified. Julian nodded and ran downstairs.

As he got changed, his mind buzzed with a million different reasons why Mrs. Demidovski could want to talk to him and none of them good. Were they taking away his scholarship? Did Mr. Yu say that his room was so messy that he wouldn't keep him in his homestay anymore? Were his grades too bad to stay in the Super Achiever's Program? (He crossed that one off the list — he'd scraped a B average in term one, and the first day of term two was too soon to be failing.) Had somebody died? Surely they would've pulled him out of class if someone had died. Maybe this was just some sort of new student — middle of the year checkup?

"What are you in a hurry for?" asked Tristan. Julian almost groaned out loud. Couldn't he do *anything* here without it being commented on?

"Mr. Yu said that Mrs. Demidovski wanted to talk to me. Is that bad?"

"Depends," said Tristan, taking the question seriously. "Could be. But I doubt it."

Julian took a deep breath and then hurriedly wiped off as much sweat as he could reach with his towel, pulled on his shirt, did up his runners, and started out the change-room door.

"Backpack," said Tristan, holding it out.

"Geez … thanks. See ya tomorrow." Julian grabbed it and ran up the stairs.

The office door was open, and Julian stepped in, holding his backpack awkwardly in one hand. "Sit down, sit down," said Mrs. Demidovski, gesturing him toward a seat.

"Thanks," said Julian nervously. Mr. Demidovski was there, too, but he wasn't paying attention to them — he was just talking to Gabriel about some papers. He still made Julian nervous, though.

"You are doing well, happy here?" Mrs. Demidovski asked.

Julian nodded. "Yes, I really like it here." He shifted his position on his chair, his legs feeling too long for the small office.

"You are friends with Taylor?" Mrs. Demidovski asked. Mr. Demidovski came and sat down beside them.

"Er, yeah?" said Julian, unsure of the correct answer.

"Girlfriend?" Mr. Demidovski asked, giving him an understanding smile.

"What? Oh, no," said Julian, not sure if he had understood him correctly. "Taylor's not my girlfriend. But we're friends."

Mr. and Mrs. Demidovski looked at each other, and Julian shuffled his foot under the chair uneasily, trying to remember any rules about dating being in the student handbook. He was pretty sure it had only said "no public displays of affection."

"You both signed up for festival doing two *pas de deux* together. That is correct?" Mr. Demidovski asked.

Julian paused, slightly unsure. "I think Taylor's mom might have signed us up?"

"Classical and contemporary ..." mused Mr. Demidovski. "Who did your contemporary *pas de deux?*" Mr. Demidovski asked suddenly. "Leah? Se-kuuu-ya? Who did for you?"

Julian's mouth fell open. "Uh, we haven't really, I mean, we haven't done it yet. Learned it."

"Must start now." Mr. Demidovski nodded firmly to himself. "Mr. Demidovski will coach you for the classical."

Julian looked at him in amazement. "Really?" he said excitedly. "But ..." His face fell as he remembered Tristan telling him how much privates with Mr. Demidovski cost. "I can't actually afford it. Me and Taylor — we were just going to sort of work on it ourselves?" Mr. Demidovski snorted in disbelief. "And so I think we'll have to do that, but it was really awesome of you to offer ..."

"Taylor, will pay hers." Said Mr. Demidovski confidently, waving away Julian's objections. "So, for you, can be free."

"Wow, thanks," said Julian. He got up a little shakily, his legs betraying him after a tiring day. "That is really, really coo— nice, of you. Thanks, Mr. Demidovski, thank you, Mrs. Demidovski."

Mr. Demidovski waved Julian's thanks away. "But you must work. Make me proud, make the school proud, yes?"

"Yes," Julian agreed.

Mr. Demidovski inclined his head toward him. "Have a good night." Mrs. Demidovski smiled and nodded at him.

Julian exited the office, closing the door behind him as quietly as possible. He gave a start of surprise — Tristan was standing in the hall waiting for him. "No ride today, so I thought I'd wait and we could bus together," he explained. "Soo ... how was it?"

Julian just grinned.

"Okay, let's ditch this place so you can tell me about it," Tristan said, shooting an uneasy glance at the office door. He swung open the door. "Come on, loser."

Chapter Two

Kaitlyn Wardle
So sore! Glad to be back at dance again and to see everyone :)

Kaitlyn woke up feeling excited, but she couldn't remember why. She lay on her bed for a moment, her covers pulled up to her chin and her eyes closed as she listened to her alarm clock beep. Oh! Today she had her first private with Mr. Moretti after class! She couldn't wait to start rehearsing for competitions. She'd already learned the variations she wanted to do, and changed them a bit to add more turns. She turned off her alarm clock and bounced out of bed, hurrying to get ready.

"Kaitlyn, are you ready?" Cecelia called upstairs.

"Almost," Kaitlyn called back. She spat out her toothpaste and washed her face, looking at it. Yay, that pimple that had started to swell on the side of her nose was fading down. Maybe it wouldn't actually appear. She ran and grabbed her ballet bag and headed downstairs.

"Kaitlyn, I need to talk to you about something," Cecelia said, too brightly.

Kaitlyn looked at her, worried. "What?" She sat down on one of the high stools at the kitchen island.

"I had a talk with Mrs. Demidovski the other day."

"Yeah?"

"They said that they are not giving you Swanhilda this year."

Kaitlyn stared at her. "But they said they were going to," she protested.

"I know. They changed their minds."

"Who's going to be Swanhilda instead of me then? Why did they change their minds?"

"I think you know why, Kaitlyn," Cecelia said pointedly. "Mrs. Demidovski said at the end of Christmas last year that you needed to lose weight, and you didn't. You had all Christmas break to lose it, and I don't think you've lost a pound." She handed a piece of paper to Kaitlyn.

Kaitlyn eyed the list in her hand warily. A lined sheet of paper filled with her mother's writing broken up only by dark bullet points, the list looked innocent enough at first glance. Kaitlyn looked up at her mother's face across from her. Cecelia looked hopeful and proud of herself. Kaitlyn glared at her, but looked down and started to read.

Goals Before Competitions Start

- Lose ten pounds
- Win Swanhilda role back by proving to the Demidovskis that you deserve it (winning at festival).
- Have privates with Mr. Demidovski

Kaitlyn was livid. "Lose ten pounds? Look, it's my body, I'll do what I want with it, all right? Just leave me alone. And of course I am going to try my best at festival, what do you think I am going to do, try to bomb it?"

Cecelia's expression grew more fixed. "Your father and I have sacrificed hours upon hours of our time on dance for you, and that's not even counting the amount of money we've paid out over the years. I've waited for you to do something about your weight all year, but obviously you aren't going to do it by yourself. You have time before competitions start. You can do this, Kaitlyn. It's all within your reach, but you have to start now."

"Just leave me alone!" Kaitlyn jumped off the couch, holding the paper clutched in her hand.

"I'm not joking. This is getting ridiculous. Do you want to be made fun of forever? It's not just about you, you know. Do you know what it feels like to go into the academy and have people like Taylor's mother give me condescending looks just because of your weight? You are better than everyone at the academy, Kaitlyn, you can do this."

"And how exactly am I supposed to get privates with Mr. Demidovski?"

"Ask him. Say you really want to be coached by him.

"Mom, that's not how it works, okay?"

"Well, I know that Taylor is going to be coached by him. Her mother was talking about it in the lobby yesterday. If you want to be the only one not coached by Mr. Demidovski, fine."

"Mom! Mr. Demidovski asks *you* if he wants to coach you, you don't ask him!"

"Kaitlyn, you have to take control of your own career."

"I am! I don't want to ask him for privates!" Kaitlyn ran for her room and slammed the door, wishing for the millionth time that she had a lock on her door. She flung herself on her bed and angrily folded the paper up into a minuscule square before sticking it into an old French-English dictionary that rested on the shelf by her bed.

"I hate her," Kaitlyn informed the ceiling. "I wish I was as skinny as Taylor …"

"Kaitlyn?" She could hear her dad knock on her bedroom door and sighed. "Kaitlyn, you need to come out now, your mother is really upset."

"Like I care!" Kaitlyn shouted back.

There was a pregnant pause, and Kaitlyn lay on her bed waiting for her parents to decide what to do.

"Kaitlyn, come out," Jeff said finally. "I'll drive you to dance."

Kaitlyn got up silently and grabbed her bag and jacket, following Jeff downstairs without looking at him or her mother.

Kaitlyn had trouble working at school at the best of times, but today it felt almost impossible. She knew she had to do school, but sometimes it seemed so stupid. Like, why did she need to know math or how electrical circuits worked if she was going to be a ballet dancer? If she had to stay at school for the amount of time the regular students did, until 3:15 or whenever it was that they finished, she'd go crazy. Finally at 11:30 a.m., the bell rang, and Kaitlyn headed out of the school. The noise level in the halls increased to epic levels as everyone spread out for lunch. Kaitlyn wasn't really sorry that she was missing lunch: she didn't want to sit there and talk to the other students. They just had nothing in common. Kaitlyn knew what she wanted to do for the rest of her life, and the other people in her grade had no idea. All they did was go to school, hang out, and do stuff recreationally. Kaitlyn thought it was stupid. She couldn't imagine not knowing what she wanted to do with her life, it would be so scary.

She broke into a run as she got out of the school doors, seeing the bus almost at the stop. Ahead of her she could see Julian and Tristan start to run, and behind her she heard Grace call, "Come on, Anna, we're going to miss it!"

They all made it on and collapsed into the seats as the bus lurched away from the stop. Julian sat down beside Taylor, and Tristan followed him, sitting on Taylor's other side. Taylor giggled happily, and Kaitlyn struggled not to roll her eyes. Taylor never seemed to get that the only reason Tristan was nice to her now was because of Julian.

"So," said Julian, grinning as he turned to Taylor, "I heard that you told Mr. Briggs you'd do a solo for the spring assembly."

Taylor squealed, and Kaitlyn winced. "*Omigawwwd*, it sucked so bad. 'Kay, so you know how Mr. Briggs has that look he does, you know the one, right?"

Tristan laughed. "Oh, the one where he pierces you with his big brown eyes and you just know that a good McKinley Dolphin would do what he's asking?"

Taylor nodded and giggled. McKinley Secondary's faculty tended to take their mascot seriously, and a good example of a McKinley Dolphin volunteered for anything and everything. Particularly if it involved a developing country, old people, the environment, or physical activity. Kaitlyn wasn't sure if it was UBC's new broad-based admissions policy that inspired so much of the student body to participate in these activities or the guilt tactics used by the McKinley staff, who all seemed to have a streak of insanity in their nature. "So. Then he totally confused me, because he was like telling me how he wanted me to perform, and I was like sure, but then he was saying, 'Good, good!' and talking about how proud of me he was and stuff, and he thought I'd said yes to this assembly." Taylor finished her sentence with a deep breath.

Julian shook his head. "Face it. Mr. Briggs is smarter than the entire student body put together. I nearly didn't drop out of French because of this story he told me about a McKinley student who helped a French tourist on the train. It was an epic story."

"Manipulative old Dolphin," Tristan said, opening up his Thermos of soup. He was bitter over the fact that Mr. Briggs had coerced Taylor into doing the performance over him. Mr. Briggs wasn't his counsellor, but still.

"So what are you going to dance?" Tristan prodded Taylor. Kaitlyn frowned, annoyed. She'd wanted to perform in the assembly. She had asked Mr. Briggs about it last semester and he had told her to check back again next semester. She had forgotten about it until now.

"I think I'm going to do my Kitri variation," Taylor prattled happily.

Kaitlyn got out her lunch bag. It felt oddly empty. She opened it up to find only a Ziploc bag of green grapes and a small container of tomato soup. Kaitlyn clenched her mouth together as she felt the corners of her eyes begin to tear up, and quickly took the bag and container out, stuffing the lunch bag back in her school bag before anyone noticed. She felt in her pocket for change; yes, she had two toonies and a couple of quarters. The problem with her bank card was that if she used it her mother would know. Even if she took out cash, her mother would see the withdrawal and ask her what she had spent it on. Kaitlyn glared at her soup as she began to eat it.

Kaitlyn ran across the street and into the JJ Bean coffee shop. Several regulars looked up in interest as she entered, not used to the speed with which she opened the door.

"And what can I get for you, Miss?" asked the barista, grinning at her. He was old, at least twenty, and his hair went in all directions, held in place by the ends of his large-framed black glasses.

Kaitlyn eyed his fish tattoo disapprovingly, and then blushed, because he would have been cute if he hadn't been old and hipster. "Can I have that cookie over there?" Kaitlyn pointed at a peanut-butter-and-chocolate cookie behind the glass, rising to her *demi-pointe* as she tried to show which one.

"The peanut butter one? Sure thing." He began to ring her up on the till. "Are you a dancer?"

"Yeah." Kaitlyn nodded.

"We get a lot of dancers in here. Do you go to that school just down the block? Uh, what's it called … don't tell me, I'll remember. Vancouver International Ballet Academy?"

"Yeah. But we just call it the academy. The academy's owners — they're kind of into big important-sounding names."

He handed her the cookie. "Well, they should be. It's a good school. I used to go to high school with a boy who went there, and man, that dude was fricking awesome!"

"What was his name?" Kaitlyn asked curiously.

"Andrew Lui?"

"Seriously?" Kaitlyn looked at him with a whole new respect. "You were friends with Andrew? That is so cool!"

"Well … I wouldn't say friends," the barista admitted. "He didn't really show up to school much. But he seemed cool."

"Oh." Kaitlyn nodded, understanding.

"Enjoy your cookie. I'm sure you need it, all you guys must burn off so many calories."

Kaitlyn blushed guiltily and left, only thinking to say thank you when she was halfway out the door. She tucked the cookie into her coat and sucked in a deep breath of cold air.

She walked in an opposite direction from the academy toward a park bench in a small city garden. She sat down and began to unwrap her cookie, thinking. It was stupid, really; her mom was right, she did need to lose weight and she was going to before competition, but it was difficult to do it when she was always hungry. *I can do this*, Kaitlyn decided firmly. She looked down. Her cookie had disappeared while she had been thinking. She brushed the crumbs off of her jeans and stood up. She checked the time; she still had half an hour to change and warm up before class. And then she had a private with Mr. Moretti! She tried to feel as excited about it as she had this morning, but she kept wondering if Mr. Moretti had influenced the Demidovskis in their decision to not cast her as Swanhilda for the June performance of *Coppelia*.

"Are you pregnant, baby?" Mr. Moretti asked, slapping Kaitlyn's stomach as he passed by her on the *barre*. Kaitlyn sucked her stomach in as she faced the *barre* diagonally to her *frappes derriere*. Across from her she could see Anna smirk. They finished the exercise and Mr. Moretti paused for a moment, deciding what to say.

"Well, that was not horrible, babies, but definitely not good."

George looked up from his piano in surprise. "What, you're not gonna tell them how bad it was? I've heard you say plenty of bad things before."

Mr. Moretti looked over at him, and grinned sarcastically. "Mrs. Demidovski says that I may not yell at the *children.*" As he said *children*, he looked at all of them, his gaze accusing. Kaitlyn shifted nervously. "All right, babies, *fondue devant, fondue a la seconde*, and ..."

Mr. Moretti called out as she went to leave after class. "Kaitlyn."

Kaitlyn turned back and walked toward him.

"You are doing competition this year, yes?"

"Yes."

"The local festivals and YAGP?"

"Yes."

"And that is why you would like to have privates with me, to work on this?"

Kaitlyn nodded.

"Well. Then we have a lot of work to do, don't we, baby?"

Kaitlyn nodded. "Yes."

"I think Gabriel has scheduled you to have a private with me this week. Let's start next week."

"Um, so I don't have a private with you this week?"

"Are you deaf? No. You don't. Go home." Kaitlyn turned around and walked out of the room, worried because maybe this meant he didn't actually want to coach her, but also relieved since he was clearly in a horrible mood. She hurried downstairs and began to get changed.

As she was at the sinks unwinding her bun, Alexandra came downstairs. "Mrs. Demidovski wants you," she said.

"Oh, okay," said Kaitlyn quickly. She shoved her hairpins and hairnet into her bag and went to go upstairs.

"Don't you have a private today with Mr. Moretti?" Alexandra asked.

"Uh ..." Kaitlyn stood in the door way, quickly thinking. "Yeah. But he didn't know, because Gabriel didn't tell him, so he couldn't coach me today. I have a private with him next week."

"Oh." Alexandra leaned over the sink, adding another layer of eyeliner.

"Who is coaching you for competition?" Kaitlyn asked.

Alexandra grinned. "Mr. Demidovski," she said. "He's coaching me and Tristan for our *pas de deux*, and then maybe a bit for our solos. I'm going to ask Mr. Yu to coach the rest of my solos."

"Mr. Yu?" Kaitlyn said, raising her eyebrows. "Really? Not Mr. Moretti?"

"Why would I ask Mr. Moretti to coach me?" Alexandra asked, staring at her. Kaitlyn stepped a bit backwards. Alexandra's eyes were a bit intimidating at times. "He doesn't like me, and I don't consider him a good teacher."

Kaitlyn shrugged. "Um, I dunno ... bye, see ya tomorrow." She turned and hurried up the stairs. She paused for a second outside of the office door, straightening her shirt. She walked in. For once, only Mrs. Demidovski was in the office. She was sitting in the only leather comfy chair in the office, and she looked up as Kaitlyn walked in. "Kailey."

"Kaitlyn," Kaitlyn corrected automatically.

"Ah, yes," said Mrs. Demidovski. "Sit down."

Kaitlyn sat.

"Mrs. Demidovski had a talk with your mother," Mrs. Demidovski said, gazing sternly at Kaitlyn, her black eyes fixed on her face.

Kaitlyn looked at her questioningly, trying to look like she had no idea what Mrs. Demidovski was talking about.

"About June performance?"

"Oh, yeah," Kaitlyn said uncomfortably. "She said something about that."

"Cannot have a Swanhilda that is too much fat," Mrs. Demidovski disgustedly. "Cannot be so. Swanhilda is a beautiful girl. That is why Franz falls in love with her."

Kaitlyn nodded quickly.

"Must lose some weight. Must be slim, slim like a strong stick. Yes?"

"Yes."

"For competition also it must be this way."

Kaitlyn nodded.

"Come here." Kaitlyn followed Mrs. Demidovski to a large wooden desk and dug around. She pulled out a small black-and-white photo and handed it to Kaitlyn. It was of an extremely skinny little girl in a white ballet dress. She was balanced *en pointe*, a small smile on her face and her arms reaching upwards in open fifth position. Her eyes were shining, and intense. "That is Mrs. Demidovski when I was younger. Not have stomach." Mrs. Demidovski laughed, patting her current rather round stomach. She took the photograph from Kaitlyn and nodded for her to sit down.

"When I was very young, eight, nine, I go to school for ballet," Mrs. Demidovski said. "I have to go away from my family. It was very hard. I missed my mother, my father, the food. But it made me strong." She looked at Kaitlyn, checking that she understood before she continued. "I was very young, I felt very homesick, sad. But then I told myself I must be good. More, I must be the best. Better than all the other girls. Every time I did the exercise, every time rehearse, I say, must be better! If is *adage,* I think, must be highest! Must be straightest! Must be most beautiful."

Kaitlyn nodded. She had never really pictured Mrs. Demidovski as a girl before, but now she thought that Mrs. Demidovski must have been just as scary back then as she was now.

"You too must be like this," Mrs. Demidovski said earnestly, grabbing her by the shoulder. "I see you dance, and I think — there is talent, yes. And the body, some problems, but can fix with diet. But where is the joy? Where is the love? Where is the passion to be best?"

Kaitlyn looked down, biting her lip. *I* do *like dancing,* she thought to herself. *I* do *want to be the best.*

"You work. You improve. Eat little, take some calcium. Don't listen to your mother, don't talk to her. I am your mother. Mrs. Demidovski is your mother here, yes?"

Kaitlyn looked at her, a little bit confused, and nodded.

"Okay. Go, go home, go to sleep. Must sleep."

"Thanks, Mrs. Demidovski." Kaitlyn left the office and stood in the hallway for a moment, confused. Taylor was talking to Keiko in the corner of the hallway as she straightened her hair in front of the mirrors, and they were both bent over giggling. Kaitlyn walked over to sit with them as she waited for her mom to come and pick her up.

Keiko was talking about Kageki. "So my mom, my stupid mom, she meets Kageki while he is visiting Tokyo in Christmastime, right?"

"Yes?" Taylor's eyes widened. "She doesn't not like Kageki, does she?"

"No, no," Keiko assured her. "He came, and she was very polite, very nice to him. Then she says, 'Is he your boyfriend?'"

"Omigod, what?" Taylor began to laugh. "Owww ..." She had accidentally pressed too close to her scalp with her hair straightener and burned herself. "Seriously, you and Kageki?"

"Yes!" Keiko continued, pleased that Taylor understood the seriousness of the situation. "I know! So ridiculous. Why are parents so strange?"

Kaitlyn laughed, and Taylor and Keiko turned around, noticing her for the first time. "See you guys later," Kaitlyn said awkwardly, seeing her mother walk toward the academy doors. She picked up her bag and walked to meet her.

"*Ja mata nee!*" Taylor called after her in a squeaky voice. Taylor and Keiko collapsed into giggles. Kaitlyn kept walking toward her mother, hoping that meant *goodbye* in Japanese. She thought it did, but she didn't know why goodbye was funny.

As they pulled into the driveway, Kaitlyn's mother finally spoke. "I put something up in your room."

"What is it?" Cecelia didn't answer, so Kaitlyn walked

slowly up the stairs with her bag. Her legs ached. She opened the door of her room: nothing looked different — she walked over to her bed and set the bag down on the bed. And saw the other side of her bedroom door.

"Are you serious?" Kaitlyn said aloud. Her mother had pinned up a chart, ready to be filled in. One column was headed with the title *Date*, and the other had *Weight.*

"It's good to visualize your progress," Cecelia explained, opening the door and coming in. "Here." She handed Kaitlyn a scale. "I got you a new one, it's for your room."

"Uh, thank you?"

"You could try to be a little more grateful! I'm going to a lot of trouble for you, you know. Most mothers wouldn't bother. And you're old enough that I shouldn't have to."

I don't want you to.

"You know this isn't my fault. You can't blame me for this."

Kaitlyn didn't answer her, and Cecelia sighed. "Fine. Just tell me, are you actually going to try?"

Kaitlyn nodded.

"Good. That's my girl. I love you, sweetie." Cecelia walked out the door, closing it behind her.

Great. Kaitlyn shoved the scale angrily under her bed and thought. Well, if she lost, like, two pounds a day, she could probably get it over with soon. That would be better than dragging it out. She quickly shed her jacket and stood on the scale, holding her breath. *Oh, geez.* She tried without her clothes on — only a half pound difference. This was so, so not okay. She sat down at her computer and Googled a BMI calculator, quickly completing it. So — probably she could lose like fifteen pounds. Yes, that would look good …

As she crawled into bed that night and turned off the light, she lay there for a while, awake and thinking. She wondered if Mrs. Demidovski had ever not wanted to be a ballet dancer. If she had ever wanted to be something else. She decided probably not: she couldn't have been Mrs. Demidovski if she had ever wanted to be anything else. *I will do this,* she decided firmly. *I will lose weight, and I will work really hard in my privates, and then they will probably give me Swanhilda again.* She rolled over and fell into a dreamless sleep.

Chapter Three

Taylor Smaylor Audley
Spring Semanar tommorow, yeeeeeeeeesssss

Taylor woke up gingerly, stretching out before she sat up, her head dizzy. Her stomach was completely empty, and as she stood up she could feel her legs shake a little. It was the first day of Spring Seminar. This was going to be great, she could feel it now. Last year had sucked, because she had been one of the worst, but she was sure she was going to be good this year. She had been working so hard, and even Mrs. Castillo had said she had gotten "a leetle bit better, yes? Leetle bit improve, need to be more, more quickly improve."

"Taylor?"

Taylor ignored her sister, busy cracking her back, her neck, her hips, and the arches of her feet. *Ah, that feels better.*

Alison came and sat on her bed, swinging her short, muscular gymnast legs off the side. Taylor had gotten the slim, tall body of her mother, but Alison was the spitting image of her father, down to the dark hair and high cheekbones, so different from Taylor's blond hair and small, round face. "What's that?" Alison asked, curious. She pointed at Taylor's chest where a sticker was stuck.

"Oops!" Taylor giggled. "I've still got it on my boob!" She peeled off a sticker with a picture of a marijuana leaf on it. "I was at this party last night, and all the guys were, like, giving out stickers to all the hot girls, so I stuck it on my boob, 'cause they were, like, only giving them to the ones they thought were hot."

"Oh, cool," said Alison, staring the sticker interestedly. "Can I have it?" she asked.

"Sure," Taylor answered, shrugging. She giggled as she pulled it off. "Ouch! Here you go."

"Was it fun?"

"Well, yeah. I mean, I think so. It was really cool, anyway."

"Taylor!" Taylor and Alison both winced as they heard their mother call up the stairs.

Taylor looked at Alison.

"You'd better go," Alison told her.

"Coming, Mom!" Taylor went out the door and down the stairs to the kitchen. "What?"

"*Don't* say, 'what' to me like that."

"I didn't say it like anything! What do you want?"

"What do I want? I want to know why you didn't come home until 1:00 a.m. the night before Spring Seminar?"

"I told you. I was going to Brandon's party."

"And I told *you*, you had to call me!"

"I forgot. Can I go now?"

Charlize sighed, putting away the bottle of vitamins she was holding. "Taylor — fine, get ready, I don't want you to be late for Spring Seminar. But we need to talk." She closed the cupboard door firmly. Taylor ran back up the stairs and started to get dressed, singing to herself as she picked out a bodysuit from the pile of dance clothes piled in the middle of her room.

"You shouldn't sing, you've got a horrible voice," Alison commented.

"Go away, your face is horrible." Taylor selected a pale blue bodysuit with black lace detailing on the front as Alison left.

"Taylor," Charlize said as she drove her downtown, "I want to talk to you, and I want you to listen to me."

"What if I don't want to listen?"

"Taylor ... you're only fifteen. You have so much time to do other things, but if you want dance, this is the time you have to work for it. If you don't give it your all now, it's going to be too late."

"I know that."

"Well, then why don't I see that you know that in your actions?"

"You do! Mom, it was just a stupid party. Drop it, okay?"

"If this is what you really want, then you are going to have to push yourself."

"Mom! Can you *please* just drop it?" Taylor stared out the window, looking out at the ocean as they drove across Granville Street Bridge. She got out her phone and began to play Sudoku on it. "It's just — these people kind of like me. And everyone at dance still is sort of mean."

"Taylor … sweetie, is it still not really better?"

"No. *They* still say the only reason I ever get anything is because of my body type."

"You've improved so much this year. Your teachers see that, I promise. It's just a couple more years, sweetie, and then you can start auditioning. Besides, this year you are doing a *pas de deux* with Julian! Isn't that going to be fun?"

"I know. It's just — it's not fair. I've been at the academy waaaaay longer than Kaitlyn."

Charlize stared at the road, thinking. "I know. But I feel like this year is going to be better for you. You just need to stay on track with dance and keep up with your school work. How is that going?"

"Good," Taylor said too quickly.

Taylor stretched in the studio assigned for warm-up at Scotiabank Dance Centre, a smile on her face. She couldn't wait to start; Spring Seminar was always so much fun. Scotiabank Dance Centre was a huge building with dance studios on multiple floors and even its own theatre. This meant that Spring Seminar was not the only thing going on in the building that day; and Taylor giggled from an upside-down bridge position as she watched a procession of middle-aged women in belly-dancing outfits pass by the doorway. She stood up and spotted Julian entering the studio. "Julian! What's up?"

"Hey, Tay." Julian set his bag down at the side and began to stretch, not looking his usual happy self.

"You okay?"

"Yeah, I'm fine, Tay," Julian assured her unconvincingly.

"You sure?"

Julian took a small breath before replying. "I'm fine. Want to stretch each other's feet?"

Taylor nodded, and stood up, standing one foot on each of Julian's arches as he held her hands to balance her.

Julian cracked a smile. "Gain some weight would you, Taylor? It'd probably improve my feet."

"Ha-ha, suuuuuuuuuure, I'll just go eat some doughnuts and have them go straight to my fat ass."

"Right, your immensely large ass," Julian said, laughing as he looked in the mirror at Taylor's reflected delicate frame. Taylor fell off his feet, caught off balance by his laughter. "Ouch." Julian rubbed his arches.

"Sorry," said Taylor guiltily.

"Not your fault."

Taylor slid into the splits beside him as he put on his soft shoes. "Have you thought about what you want our *pas de deux* to be?"

"Yeah," Julian said. "I like black swan ..."

Taylor stared at him, horrified.

"I was joking!" Julian said, laughing. "I know we aren't good enough for it. It's cool. I don't really know ... I like *Le Corsaire*, but maybe Mr. Demidovski will pick."

"Yeah, probably," Taylor agreed. "But it's cool to think about it."

Kaitlyn had come in behind them. "Mr. Demidovski?" she said, looking confused. "You guys are both having privates with Mr. Demidovski?"

I don't like her bun, Taylor thought critically, looking at it. It was combed straight back without a part, and the perfectly round circle lay in the exact centre of the back of her head. She'd tied a red-and-white polka-dot ribbon to it that stood out on her thick, pale brown hair, not looking particularly attractive against her very white skin.

"Yeah," Julian answered Kaitlyn. "Mr. Demidovski's coaching us, so we thought he might be deciding which *pas de deux* we do."

"I didn't know that you guys were even doing a *pas de deux* together."

"Yeah, we decided before Christmas," Julian explained. "Who's coaching you?"

"Oh …" Kaitlyn took her time sitting down and setting her bag beside her. "I haven't really decided."

"Cool."

"By the way, guess what I just found out?" Kaitlyn asked, brightening up.

"Mother Mother is playing an underage show on Saturday?" Julian guessed.

"No," Kaitlyn said, confused. "We have Theresa Bachman for ballet class."

"Cool!" Julian paused for a moment, thinking, then asked sheepishly, "Who's Theresa Bachman?"

Taylor and Kaitlyn both turned to him, shocked. "You don't know who Theresa Bachman is?" Taylor said loudly, her eyes huge.

"Julian!" Kaitlyn said, as if he had just said something deeply sacrilegious.

"What?" Julian protested. "Just tell me, who is she?"

"Only one of Canada's most famous ballerinas in, like, history," Taylor said. "I can't believe you haven't heard of her!"

"She used to dance for Vancouver Ballet until she retired last year," Kaitlyn continued. "I'm sure you've heard of her. You can't not have heard of her."

Julian shrugged. "I don't know, dude. I guess I just don't pay attention to that stuff."

The long white bony knobs of Theresa's feet made Taylor want to puke. Her toes had been shoved to an acute angle by a humongous bunion on her big toe, and it was as if her toes were going in a different direction than her feet. Theresa smiled toothily up at the circle of students surrounding her as they stared at her feet. She stretched them out, showing them off proudly.

"What do you have to do to your *pointe* shoes to make it so you can stand in them?" Taylor asked her curiously.

"Quite a bit," Theresa answered. "Do you want to see?"

The students nodded enthusiastically, so Theresa brought her duffle bag into the centre of the room, and reached in to pull out a large canvas bag. She spilled the contents on the floor, and the students automatically drew closer. Taylor reached over Julian's leg and tentatively held her hand over one pair. "Can I look at it?" she asked Theresa.

Theresa visibly winced, but then handed Taylor a different pair. "Here. You can touch *these* ones!" Theresa smiled brightly at her, and Taylor unfolded the shoes.

They were neatly tucked inside each other with the ribbons wrapped around. Taylor unwrapped the ribbon carefully, checking the size — a pair of 4 Xs. The Freed Classics were completely bent and the portion of the box where Theresa's bunion lay had been completely worn down to the point where there was no box left, just canvas and satin. "So cool," Taylor said.

"All right, let's get back to class," Theresa said. Taylor handed her back the shoes and went back to the *barre*.

"Not many people have good posture," Theresa said, looking around, frowning. "Come back to the centre. Lie down on your back."

They obeyed.

"Now, try to stretch out your back and let every part of it touch the ground. Each vertebrae."

"My butt is getting in the way," Taylor whispered, wiggling as she tried to accomplish what Theresa asked.

"Well, then chop it off," someone whispered back. Taylor started to giggle and couldn't stop, so she sat up to watch Theresa do it.

"Like this," she explained, lying with her legs bent and turned out, every part of her back on the ground.

"Yes, but she doesn't have a butt," Julian complained beside Taylor.

"Yes," Taylor agreed. "I don't think this is going to work for us."

One by one the other students sat up, looking sheepish. "I did it," Jessica informed them.

Great, Taylor thought, rolling her eyes. *Three points to the anorexic.* She looked over at Julian, and realized that he was thinking the same thing. They both started giggling.

"Now, let's go do some centre work," Theresa said hesitantly. She didn't seem at all sure of her class syllabus.

Alexandra put up her hand. "Ms. Bachman —"

"Call me Theresa," Theresa assured her. "No one ever calls me Ms. Bachman. It makes me feel old."

The class giggled nervously: Theresa was almost fifty years old. "Theresa," Alexandra began again. "How come you decided to leave the Vancouver Ballet?"

Theresa looked sad, and Taylor wished Alexandra hadn't asked that question.

"It wasn't really my decision," Theresa informed them, smiling unhappily. "I was given a choice, retire, or — be let go."

"But why?" Alexandra persisted. Taylor winced.

"Because," said Theresa. "They wanted to move in a different direction with the company, and I wasn't a part of their vision."

"Why? Was it a different style or something?"

"Yes. Younger." Theresa laughed. "New generation in the company, they couldn't find roles for me. Well, they could have if they'd tried, but they decided to just move on instead."

There was a widespread sigh.

"I'm fine with it," Theresa assured them unconvincingly. "It's time for a new path. And I've started teaching — you are my first class, as a matter of fact!"

"You've never taught before?" Kaitlyn exclaimed.

"No," Theresa admitted, hugging her legs into her chest as she looked at the circle of students surrounding her. She had dressed in dance clothes to teach them, a pale yellow bodysuit, black tights, and a flowered wrap skirt, and before she had taken them off she had been wearing canvas shoes. If it weren't for the wrinkles and lines on her body, she could have passed for one of her students in size and attire.

Taylor bit her lip. She was worried for Theresa, she was telling them too much; teachers needed to keep their distance, otherwise the class wouldn't run properly. And this was only the first day.

"I like that we are getting to know each other," Theresa said. "I think this is a good idea. I think I could teach you a lot just by answering your questions — your regular teachers already teach you technique, but I can answer any other questions you have."

Alexandra put her hand up again. "How do you do your hair?"

Theresa patted the French roll that her hair was firmly bound in. "I can teach you and whoever else wants to learn on your lunch break if you want."

"Awesome!" Julian said loudly.

Everyone turned around to look at Julian and his newly cut hair, and began to laugh.

"You can come, too — Julian," Theresa said, reading his name tag. "But this might be a bit difficult for *your* hair. It looks a little short."

"Who was your favourite partner?" Tristan asked suddenly from the back.

"Who was that?" Theresa asked, sitting up so she could see him. "A boy!" She looked excited. "I love it when the men take an interest in partnering," she explained. "So many male dancers, they just don't work in that area of their dancing. Which I find foolish. The old ballets, they don't really have well-fleshed-out male leads, and the men really have to focus on the partnering. So many fine young male dancers can get ahead by being a good partner and dancing with a more established female lead."

Tristan nodded, a little embarrassed. He'd already come to the same conclusion, but it was an entirely different matter to have it told so bluntly in front of the class.

"My favourite partner — let's see," Theresa said, sitting back as she considered. The last of the students that had been standing to keep warm in case they were going back to the *barre* sat, and Taylor adjusted her position a bit so she was sitting closer to Julian and could feel the heat from his body. It was a cold spring in Vancouver that year, despite the sun. Julian had told Taylor that it was probably global warming, which didn't make sense to Taylor, but she let it go — science frequently didn't make sense to her. Besides, Julian tended to get over-emotional and boring when he started talking about things like the environment.

"Well, I guess I would have to pick Isaac," Theresa decided. "Isaac — he was a bit younger than me, and a very good partner. We never really matched well in the studio: he never wanted to rehearse as much as I did, so in that way we didn't suit. But our style of dancing, what we were trying to achieve artistically, was very cohesive."

"Did you ever fight about how much you rehearsed?" Tristan asked.

"Yes!" Theresa laughed. "All the time. That's why the company stopped pairing us together — he didn't take criticism well either."

Taylor giggled. She could picture Theresa obsessively scolding some partner over the correct way to lift her.

"He had awful timing, as well," Theresa said, reminiscing. "I have excellent timing, so that was always difficult. It was hard to be tactful at times, and of course he was very sensitive."

"How would you tell him his timing was off then?" Tristan asked.

"Hmm — this one time we were rehearsing a lovely piece to set to Handel, and he kept lifting me up on the upbeat when it should have been the down. It was awful, because you would hear this definitive down" — Theresa hit the floor with her foot — "and then he would lift me. It completely ruined the choreography. So I told him," Theresa started to giggle, and they giggled along with her. "I told him — oh dear. I said: 'Isaac, we are not leaving this studio until you lift me up on the right count.' He was not impressed, but we stayed in the studio for three hours until he got it right. Then he stormed out and went and got drunk, he was hungover for class the next day. He knew I would've complained to the artistic director if he hadn't stayed." Theresa shook her head, smiling dreamily as if recalling a fond memory.

"Poor Isaac," Taylor whispered to Julian.

"Do you mean Isaac Claire?" Alexandra asked, wide eyed.

Theresa covered her mouth. "Yes. Don't tell him I said that. He is a very sweet man, and I'm sure he's more mature now — we didn't really keep in touch after he left the company, apart from writing a few times. Now he choreographs. His work is a bit mechanical for my taste, but he's doing well."

Taylor giggled. It was so cool to hear gossip about ballet dancers that she looked up to. Theresa looked like she was having fun, too. Taylor had the odd impression that Theresa really wanted them to like her, as if their approval meant something to her. Which Taylor found strange; why would one of the most treasured Canadian ballet dancers of her time care what a class of young students thought of her?

"Did you ever have sex with any of your dance partners?" There was a sudden hush, and everyone turned to look at Delilah. "What? I was just curious."

"Oh my God, Delilah," Alexandra said shaking her head, embarrassed.

Delilah shrugged.

They turned back to Theresa to see if she would answer. "Well, yes, a few," Theresa answered to their surprise. "But I found that the extra layer of complication that added was harmful to our ballet partnership, so I stopped doing that."

Taylor didn't know what to think of that statement. It sounded perfectly logical, and more than a little odd at the same time. She wanted to be a ballet dancer who was as amazing as Theresa, but she hoped she wouldn't be so strange when she was.

"Did you ever think of leaving the company?" Julian asked. "Dancing in a different one? I know you did some guest stuff, but ..."

"Not a lot of guesting," Theresa filled in for him. "And yes, I did think of leaving for a different company. I got offers for bigger companies that would have made me more of a name internationally, but honestly I just couldn't do it. Vancouver Ballet is — was — my home, my safety net."

"So you were happy there," Kaitlyn prodded.

"Yes," Theresa said hesitantly. "Yes — yes, I was. I was happy there. I was surrounded by so many people who wanted me to do well, you see, and I needed that support system. Some companies are big and make dancers stars, but with Vancouver Ballet it was the other way around. I put them on the map. So they needed me, and I needed them — until they didn't need me anymore, of course."

There was silence. No one really knew what to say.

After they finished class, Taylor hurried, wanting to catch up to Julian before he left. It was difficult, because the boys always took far less time to get changed than the girls. She found him sitting on a bench, texting. "Julian!"

"Hey, Tay," Julian said, not looking up. "How do you spell 'superficial'?"

"I don't know," Taylor said, sitting down beside him. "I have dyslexia, I can't spell. What are you trying to write?"

Julian passed her his phone. "This," he sighed. "I'm trying to tell my friend Caspian that he shouldn't be dating this girl because she is really annoying and superficial. But my phone's spell check won't work."

Taylor looked at the screen. "Just send this," she suggested. "He'll probably understand what 'superphicial' means."

"Ah, here, got it," Julian said suddenly taking the phone back. "It's an f. I'm an idiot." He pressed Send.

"Anyway," Taylor said, "I was wondering, you still want to do two *pas de deux* with me, right?"

"Yeah, of course!" Julian replied, surprised. "Like, I worked on the contemporary *pas de deux* we're going do on Christmas break and everything."

"Yay," said Taylor."Hey … do you want to maybe go back in the studio and rehearse?" She looked at Julian hopefully. "I really, really, really want to see the *pas de deux* you choreographed. I am actually so stoked."

Julian looked around. There was an empty studio in front of them. He grinned. "Yeah. Come on." They both ran into the large studio, giggling. Taylor did a cartwheel in the middle of the room. "The whole studio, for us!" she said happily.

Julian set up the music.

"I like this *pas de deux*," Taylor said, as she and Julian lay on the floor, panting. "It's so fast and fun. I like that better than slow and serious dances." Taylor and Julian looked up, hearing a noise in the doorway.

Theresa was standing there, dressed in her street clothes. "What have you been doing?" she asked.

"Uh ... fooling around, choreographing," said Julian carelessly, ruining the effect immediately by blushing.

"Choreographing what?" demanded Theresa as she walked closer to them. "You like choreographing?" Her eyes were focused on Julian, and Taylor scooted a little bit away from him.

"A ... just a *pas de deux*... it's sort of stupid, but I like choreographing, you know?" said Julian. "It's just so ... so much fun."

"Show me?" asked Theresa.

At that moment Julian's cell began to ring. Taylor turned it off for him. "It's Tristan," she said, grimacing.

"Oh, yeah, we have that RAD class today!" Julian said, horrified. "I totally forgot about it. I can't go now, there's not enough time."

Taylor turned Julian's phone to silent.

"Do you think I could see some of your choreography? If you don't mind?" Theresa asked Julian.

"Um, sure," said Julian, cracking his feet on the floor nervously. "Do you think you could turn on the music for us? That button. Thanks!"

He walked over to the centre of the room and stood next to Taylor, waiting. Theresa pushed Play.

Julian finished the *pas de deux* not terribly well, as he suddenly remembered that Theresa was watching him and might think that his choreography was weird, and he left the floor muttering, "Not very good of course, it's just for fun, you know? Kind of stupid, I know."

But the beginning and middle were good enough for Theresa to sit up even straighter in order to pay better attention and to exclaim when he had finished, "You really are talented! How long have you been working on this?"

Julian shot a glance at Taylor: he had told her that he had been working on it since Christmas break, but he had really just finished choreographing most of it today, and the first half the night before. "I've been working on it for — um, a little while."

"You really do have talent," Theresa said excitedly. "We have to talk tomorrow. I think I have an idea." She left the room, smiling, and lost in her own world. Julian stared after her, confused.

As soon as she left, Taylor turned to Julian. "That was so random," she whispered, staring after Theresa. "But, she's right. You are really good at choreographing! And you dance so much better when you are dancing your own work. This *pas de deux* is way better than any of the academy's contemporary teachers have ever done that I've seen. It's more like Leah's. But different. I really, really like it! What is that song? I recognize it."

"It's 'Sail,'" said Julian, his grin lighting up his whole face. "That Awolnation song? Thanks." He sat down and stretched, out of breath.

"You need to dance like that more often," said Taylor disapprovingly. "Full-out, I mean."

"I'm just out of breath because I'm not doing soccer and stuff anymore," Julian protested.

"You should be totally in shape if you've been taking class properly," said Taylor. But she let it go. "Theresa's right, you're, like, really good. We should definitely do what you choreographed for competition!"

"Do we have to ask the Demidovskis?" Julian asked.

"Yes," said Taylor, frowning. "But — let's say we got a contemporary teacher to choreograph it for us. They'd panic if you told them you did it."

"Yeah," said Julian agreed. "They totally would. Okay."

"Okay, let's work on this," Taylor said firmly. "Nobody's waiting in the hall, so we can use this studio until someone kicks us out. We just have to check the hallway every so often to make sure no one is out there waiting."

By the time they got out of the studio it was dark, but it had stopped raining. Julian had learned the choreography to the *Le Corsaire pas de deux* and they had both learned exactly how hard they would have to work to get it ready for festival, they had both rehearsed their respective variations once (well, Julian three-quarters as he forgot bits of it) and they had experimented enough for Julian to get an idea of what changes he had to make to their contemporary *pas de deux* to make it work. Dancing with Taylor when he was choreographing in his brain was quite different from actually dancing with Taylor, and some of the lifts and ideas he had just didn't translate into real life. They were both completely exhausted, but extremely happy.

"I am so tired, but I'm glad I finally got to see your choreography," said Taylor, almost skipping as they walked to the bus stop.

"Me too," said Julian, marking steps to music in his head. "Do you think Theresa actually liked my work?"

"I think so," said Taylor, yawning. "Yay, bus!"

Chapter Four

Alexandra Dunstan
"You have a face for the radio, But I know you'd like to see it in a show ..." haha, love The View, ultimate insult.

It was warm in the studios before class, and Alexandra could see the sun streaming through the windows onto the grey dance floor. It was pretty, and her body felt warm and loose after warming up. She rolled over and rose up into a bridge, grabbing her ankles and trying to straighten so her body was completely bent in half.

"Almost," said Tristan admiringly. He tried himself, but wasn't flexible enough to touch his ankles. He flopped down on the floor again in a pout. "It's just because you're a girl," he informed Alexandra.

She rolled her eyes. "Sure," she answered. Tristan pulled a Kleenex out of his tights and blew his nose. "Ew," said Alexandra.

"What? I have a cold," said Tristan. "Where would you rather I put my Kleenex? Or would you like me to have snot flying out my nose during pirouettes?"

"Oh, do you have a coke problem?" asked Alexandra, starting to giggle again.

"Huh?" asked Tristan, confused.

"Gelsey Kirkland, in her autobiography," Alexandra explained. "It's one of my favourite dance biographies. It's called *Dancing on My Grave.*"

"Nice," snorted Tristan. Alexandra ignored him.

"Anyway, she writes about how snot used to fly out of her nose when she did *fouettes* and stuff on stage after she started doing coke."

"Didn't anyone notice?" asked Tristan in disbelief.

"Apparently not," said Alexandra, shrugging. "They just said she was getting better all the time. They only started to do something about it when she started missing class and performances and stuff."

"Typical," said Tristan, shaking his head. "People are so stupid. Can you loan me that book sometime?"

"Sure," said Alexandra. "What time is it?"

Tristan looked at his cellphone. "Time for class."

Alexandra stretched out her legs and arms like a starfish, yawning. She didn't want to get up off the floor: her body was so flexible and warm that it melted on the hard rubber ground. The first warm day of the year. She got up in one rush of motion and grabbed her bag. "Let's go then." They walked to the elevator and got on, the first students to leave. Alexandra punched the button and leaned back on the elevator wall as they began their descent to the bottom floor. "How's Deer?"

"What?"

"Your Julian. He's been out of it all week, I figured you'd know what was going on with him."

"How should I know? He doesn't tell anyone anything. And he's not my Julian."

"Why are you mad at him?"

"I'm not mad at him!"

"Whatever you say."

"How come you called him *deer*?"

"D-E-E-R." Alexandra spelled out the word. "Because he looks like one if you confuse him, and I think that should be his new nickname. I asked him what summer schools he was auditioning for yesterday and he just stood there looking blank." They got off the elevator and walked toward the studio, passing dancers from a contemporary company that rehearsed upstairs.

"Yeah, I don't really know what is up with him. I asked him if he wanted to go to auditions with me, and he was just acting really weird." Tristan pushed open the door and walked inside the large studio. They put their bags down in the middle-front of the room and carried a centre *barre* out to use. Alexandra began to *develope a la seconde* and held it. "That's a lot higher," Tristan commented admiringly.

Alexandra smiled. "Thanks." She looked in the mirror — she still wasn't strong enough, and her extensions weren't high enough. They were higher, and if she just kicked them up, she could get the height she wanted: but she wasn't strong enough at that height to *develope* her legs properly; not without cheating.

The other students began to run in, too late to get the best spots as usual, as Alexandra and Tristan had already taken them. In a few minutes the studio was full of ballet students, from the academy and other schools around B.C.

Looking at the clock, Alexandra saw that Theresa was a bit late. She hung her back down over the *barre* to stretch it out, watching the dancers around her as she did so. Two *barres* down, Kaitlyn was laughing with one of the girls from her old school. Alexandra frowned. She really hoped that Kaitlyn wouldn't get Swanhilda for June show. Otherwise she would just be even more insufferable. This morning she had been telling Michael and Chloe about the time that she had played Clara at only ten years old. Alexandra had wanted to interrupt to point out that the reason she had played Clara was that she had danced at a recreational school and was pretty much the only good dancer at the school.

Theresa walked in, setting her many bags at the front of the classroom. Alexandra saw her look over and smile at Julian and Taylor. She frowned: what was that about? Did they know Theresa already somehow? She took out her Thera-Band and began to stretch her leg extensions with it.

Theresa walked to the front of the room and clapped her hands together for class to start. "Good morning everyone!" she said excitedly. "Shall we begin?" She began to give them a *plie* exercise, but it was obvious that her attention was elsewhere. She stopped in front of Taylor and ran her finger along her leg as Taylor *tendued* to the side. "There. This is simply beautiful. Gorgeous, my darling, this is a lovely line."

The pianist seemed to be hitting the keys a little harder than usual and Alexandra could feel herself snapping all her movements in response, making them jerky and awkward instead of fluid and elastic. "Let's do something a little different today with the music," Theresa said suddenly, wincing at the closing notes of the *tendue* exercise. "Mary, do you think you could play some Christmas music?"

"It's April," Alexandra whispered to Tristan.

Tristan shrugged. "That is irrelevant," he whispered back. "I want some Christmas music."

Theresa walked over to the piano and began humming "Deck the Halls."

"Oh!" Theresa gave a start of surprise as some of the ladies of the Vancouver Ballet Society came in to watch. She hadn't yet gotten used to them dropping in to view classes. "We are just about to listen to some lovely Christmas music!"

They smiled politely as Mary began to play, hitting the keys even harder. Theresa began to choreograph a *frappe* exercise to the carol, and the class marked along with her. Alexandra smiled: there was something about the discordant combination of sun pouring through the windows and Christmas music being thumped out of a piano that made her very happy. Theresa came over to her and grabbed her leg, jerking it in and out while holding her knee at a solidly turned-out angle. She let go and Alexandra attempted to mimic what Theresa's hand had forced her to do, but she couldn't quite manage it.

"Almost," Theresa assured her. Alexandra smiled at her, grateful to receive some positive corrections, but almost immediately Theresa moved on to work with

Julian. "Much better," she gushed. Alexandra frowned and her smile dropped as she began to work harder.

As she worked, she looked in the mirror in front of her, shooting glances throughout the exercise with her eyes as her head moved with her arm the way it was supposed to. Nothing was good enough yet. Not for competition, not for getting a position with a company. Her arches weren't strong enough yet; she couldn't consistently roll through smoothly; her arms were awkward when she was nervous; and her legs, although flexible, were nowhere near strong enough. Let alone the right size. Her thighs *still* looked huge. She looked across at Taylor, and bit her lip. It didn't matter that Taylor was messing up the exercise every few seconds, or that she had sloppy technique, Theresa would still correct her because she had a good body type. Leonie Camden had had a good body type. *What is wrong with you, Alexandra?* She asked herself between *grand battements. I need to get better. I need to lose weight. I need to be skinnier than Taylor, and stronger than Kaitlyn, and they are both younger than me.* With every goal she set she *grand battemented* a little higher and more violently, and on the last one she got stuck up in the air, nearly throwing out her back and coming down a count late.

"Easy, careful!" said Theresa, appearing behind her and patting her on the shoulder with a bony hand. She jabbed her finger in Alexandra's stomach. "You have to work on this being stronger, your back is very loose and it needs to be supported."

Alexandra nodded and wiped away the sweat that was dripping down her forehead.

Alexandra didn't bother changing out of her wet dance clothes, instead slipping a dress overtop of her tights and bodysuit and slipping on her leather boots. She could feel the sweat from her bodysuit seeping through to the fabric of her dress. *Grooosss ...*

"You're in a hurry," Grace commented, leisurely brushing out her thick light brown hair in front of the change-room mirror.

Alexandra looked up from tying her boots. "Yeah. Tristan and I have a private with Mr. Demidovski."

"Oh. Yeah, you're doing all those competitions, right?" Grace looked condescending. "I guess that makes sense, for you."

Alexandra stopped in the middle of picking up her bag. "What do you mean, 'for me'?"

"Well, it's like going to be hard for you to get a job, right? You're going to need like a reeaaallly good resume, with lots of medals and stuff."

"Uh, everyone does. That's kinda how you get a visa."

"Well, not everyone," said Grace delicately. She smiled at Alexandra through the mirror as she rummaged through her makeup bag. "I mean, I don't do competitions, and the Demidovskis never told me that I should do them."

Alexandra stared at her, disbelieving. "They never told you to do them because you suck at competitions!"

Anna came out of a stall, her eyes wide. "Wow. Defensive much?"

Grace's eyes began to tear up. "I can't believe you said that to me," she sniffled. Anna passed her a wad of toilet paper.

"God, Alexandra, you are such a bitch!"

Alexandra stared at the tableau in front of her. No words came to her rescue. "You know what — just — I don't even know. I have to get to my private. Because I *work* at dance? Instead of just resting on being a favourite?" she finished angrily, walking out of the bathroom and swinging her bag onto her back. The door was the heavy kind that takes a while to close and closes with a slow wheeze when it does, so Alexandra didn't even get the satisfaction of slamming it. Instead, she ran down the stairs instead of taking the elevator in order to stomp down the cement steps. It made her feel slightly better, and as she walked out the front doors she said, "Bye!" to the receptionist.

She pushed open the big glass doors and took a deep breath in. Fresh air was so much better after leaving a sweaty studio. The sunshine was misleading, as it was still cold outside, and the wind was swirling everything upwards. A newspaper was drifting lazily across the street, and Alexandra turned sharply around to walk to the bus stop. "Agh! Omigod, sorry!" Alexandra had accidentally run straight into Theresa. She stepped backwards, her eyes wide with the horror of it. "I'm so sorry!"

Theresa laughed. She looked more amused than angry. "That's fine."

"Um, see you tomorrow in class. Thank you. Geez. Sorry." Alexandra continued on her way, her face red and her steps stiff as she tried to regain her dignity. To make matters worse, it appeared that Theresa was also going that way.

"Are you walking to the bus stop?" Theresa asked brightly.

"Yeah," said Alexandra, falling back to match Theresa's pace.

"Which way are you going?"

Alexandra pointed. "I'm going to my normal school to have a private," she explained.

"Oh? Which school is that?"

"The Vancouver International Ballet Academy? But everyone just calls it the academy. People who know it, I mean. It's a super-long name, like nobody calls it that but the Demidovskis, because they named it that —" Alexandra stopped talking, realizing that she was babbling.

Theresa smiled calmly. "Yes, I know the academy," she said. "I admire some of their training — not all of their methods, but they have produced some very good dancers. I'm going there myself."

"What, really?" Alexandra said. As soon as she had spoken she realized that she had sounded rude, and so she added: "That's nice, it's really a very nice school." She wanted very badly to ask why Theresa was visiting the academy, but she thought that would probably be rude, and so she forced herself not to.

The bus pulled up to the stop, and Theresa and Alexandra got on. Alexandra walked behind Theresa, unsure what she was supposed to do. Should she sit next to Theresa? Or would Theresa not want her to? Theresa sat down on one of the benches, and seeing Alexandra start to head toward the back of the bus, she patted the seat beside her, saying: "You can sit next to me. I really don't take up that much room, you know."

Alexandra sat. Carefully. She set her bag down in her lap slowly, being careful not to hit Theresa with it. Alexandra had never sat on a bus with posture that good in her entire life.

"Do you know the two students in your class, Julian and Taylor?" Theresa asked casually as the bus pulled away from the stop. "Are they in your class at the academy?"

"Uh, yes," said Alexandra, glad of something to talk about. "Julian Reese and Taylor Audley, they're in my class … my class has several levels in it. It's not that big of a school."

"How old are they?" Theresa asked, staring at Alexandra intently.

"Well, um, Taylor's just turned fifteen, I think, and Julian's my age, so like, fifteen turning sixteen?"

"That's good," said Theresa, nodding approvingly. "That's a very good age."

Alexandra sat there, a bit confused and a bit hurt that Theresa had asked about Julian and Taylor. "Uh, yeah." The bus pulled up in front of the academy and Alexandra got up, stepping backwards so that Theresa could exit first and then following her up to the school.

The academy had once been a church, then had

been a community centre, and had finally been bought by the Demidovskis. It was an impressive building, with a stone exterior and wood inside, and the entryway had a beautiful stained-glass picture of a female dancer kneeling under a tree to put on her *pointe* shoes and a male ballet dancer standing behind her holding on to the tree. Alexandra loved the academy's building, but she rarely looked at it from the outside. The inside was falling apart, with plumbing that was always broken and a roof that constantly dripped so it was easy to forget the beauty amid the daily annoyance. But walking up to the school, Alexandra saw it as Theresa must be seeing it, as the beautiful old building that it was, and she felt proud.

"It's gorgeous," Theresa whispered, standing to admire the doorway before she walked in. Alexandra smiled. Inside there was an onslaught of noise, with little kids running around everywhere, and mothers standing around awkwardly taking up space.

"The little kids always have extra festival practice during spring break," Alexandra said, shrugging.

"Which way is the office?"

Alexandra pointed at the door through the maze of pink bodysuits and sparkle-clothed children. Theresa made her way in that direction, and Alexandra continued down the hall toward the change rooms. She wondered why on earth Theresa wanted to stop by the academy. *Oh! She probably knows the Demidovskis*, she decided suddenly. With that she hurried into the change rooms, stuffing her bag and clothes in her locker and pulling out a pair of *pointe* shoes, her toe tape, and her CD. She hurried upstairs again to put on her *pointe* shoes. It felt like there was absolutely nowhere to sit, and she found herself huddled in the corner as she taped her toes. *Ugh.* All the sweat on her body had gone cold and there was no time to change her bodysuit. She tried to warm her feet up quickly, and then looked at the clock again: it was time. She headed upstairs to the top studios where her private had been scheduled. Her stomach felt weird, like it was turning in and out and around, and when she sucked it in, it felt too full, so she went into the upstairs bathroom and locked the door behind her. The toilet was old, and chipped in places. She quickly threw up the remains of her tomato soup. There. That was better. When she held her hands around her waist the space between her hands was the one she was used to. She flushed the toilet, which looked quite disgusting with the red soup against the white bowl, and took a deep breath in. The water she washed her mouth and hands with was cold, and it felt good against her hot face. She left the bathroom and walked back to the studio, feeling a little better.

Tristan was already stretching at the doorway. He looked up, surprised. "You're almost late," he commented.

"I had to take the bus. But what are doing here?"

"Mr. Demidovski changed your private with Mr. Yu to a private for both of us with him," Tristan explained. "Mr. Yu's not feeling well."

The door opened and Mrs. Castillo came out, ushering out a scared-looking nine-year-old girl. Her mother was waiting in one of the chairs and quickly stood up.

"What are you feeding her?" Mrs. Castillo asked abruptly, her hand on the little girl's shoulder.

The mother looked confused.

"For example, lunch. What do you pack her for lunch?" Mrs. Castillo asked the woman impatiently.

"Um, a sandwich, and yogurt, and —"

"What is in the sandwich? Peanut butter?" Mrs. Castillo pressed her hand against the girl's stomach and gestured impatiently for her mother to come over. "See? I press, and in. Mushy, mushy. The other girls in her class, they do not have this problem. See the good ones, see Violet, in her class or Chloe, a bit older, but still slimmer than her." Mrs. Castillo pushed the girl's stomach in once more. "You see?"

The girl's mother looked like she was about to cry. "Yes, yes, I understand."

"I will talk to you about what she should eat," Mrs. Castillo said firmly.

Alexandra and Tristan slipped into the studio. It was five minutes after the time their private should have started. "Do you have the music?" Alexandra asked. "I only have the music for my variation."

"Yeah, course," Tristan shrugged. He walked over and put it in the CD player. "Want to run through it once before Mr. Demidovski comes?"

"Sure." Alexandra stood up, testing out her ankle. It was still extremely weak — it had been bothering her for a while, but she kept hoping it would get better. It would be completely fine, but then sometimes she would step on *pointe* and it would just give out under her, or sharp jabbing pains, warm like electricity, would shoot up from her foot.

Tristan turned to her before he put the CD in. "Hey," he began nervously. "Lexi, I was wondering, do you want to go shopping with me after class tomorrow? Julian's birthday is coming up and I wanted to get him a present."

"Yeah, but you're the one that's friends with him," said Alexandra. "I mean, is he even doing anything for his birthday? I wasn't invited to anything."

"Well, Taylor's having a surprise birthday party for him. And she was probably too scared to invite you, so ..."

"*Taylor's* arranging it?"

"Yeah. She's going way overboard, too, you know what she's like. She actually wrote me a list of stuff that Julian would probably like. In purple gel pen."

"That's stupid. It's not like she's his only friend. I mean, it's kind of insulting saying that she knows better than you do what Julian would like, you both probably spend around the same amount of time with him."

"Exactly. She's totally going nutso over it."

"Are Grace and Anna invited?"

"Uh, no? Neither Taylor or Julian are friends with Grace and Anna. So, will you come?"

Alexandra deliberated for a second. "Sure. Why not."

Tristan smiled, his face lighting up. "Yay. This is going to be so much more fun now that you are coming. I was expecting it to be awful, dealing with Taylor by myself for that long."

"For what, a couple of hours?"

"Uh … it's a sleepover. At her house."

"Tristan, you didn't say —"

At that moment Mr. Demidovski walked in. "I apologize," he said placing his fingers on his heart. "I apologize, I am late. Are you warmed up? The muscles are good, yes?"

Alexandra and Tristan nodded. Gabriel followed Mr. Demidovski through the door, carrying his black old leather bag and setting it beside him. Mr. Demidovski slowly unravelled his woollen plaid scarf and took off his Burberry coat, hanging it beside him, and then sitting down, slowly, dramatically, with the air of a performer who knows exactly how much time he is taking with every movement.

"So? What *pas de deux* have you picked? Come on, come on, don't keep Mr. Demidovski waiting."

"We picked *Sleeping Beauty*," Tristan said. "We've got the music …"

"*Sleeping Beauty* — yes, yes, maybe a good fit. Let me see." Gabriel went over and turned the CD player on as Tristan and Alexandra got ready. Alexandra could feel her heart pounding, her palms sweaty with nerves. Dancing for Mr. Demidovski was like going on stage in itself. The academy students made fun of the Demidovskis on a daily basis, but the truth is they respected them very much. How could Alexandra not be nervous dancing for Mr. Demidovski when all she had to do was look at the pictures of him downstairs when he was younger — or his movements now — to know how good he had been? It was better to be yelled at by Mr. Demidovski than ignored, and Alexandra was thrilled that he had finally scheduled a private with her, even if it was shared with Tristan.

The music began to play, and Alexandra *releved* in fifth position, *developed* her right leg *devant*, and then took a *port de bras* backwards. This *pas de deux* suited them both very well, and Alexandra loved dancing it with Tristan. He was annoying, but they had very similar timing and style. Alexandra didn't have to think so much about dancing with Tristan as she did if she was partnered with any of the other boys. If they messed up while dancing with each other it was a failure of technique, not communication.

When they had finished, Mr. Demidovski sat in his chair silently for a moment, assembling the right words. "It is — if I am the judge," he said slowly: "It is 10 percent. The work, the technical is 10 percent."

Alexandra's face fell, and she could feel Tristan's do the same beside her. She nodded, quickly.

"The artistic. The emotion. It is better — maybe 70 percent."

Alexandra smiled. It had felt good when she had been dancing it.

"Must be better." Mr. Demidovski slowly drew one of his black, sock-covered feet out of his black dress shoes. He pointed it in front of him, his long toes and foot bony and still arched. "See? My foot — my foot it is gorgeous. My arch it is beautiful. I am old. You should be many, many times better. Yes?"

"Yes," Alexandra and Tristan chorused.

Mr. Demidovski slipped his foot back into his shoe and rolled up his sleeves. He nodded to Gabriel that he could go back to the office. "We have much work to do," Mr. Demidovski said happily. "Now, first, Christian, show me your *jeté*. It is not charming." Tristan ran back to the corner to show him.

As Tristan and Alexandra left the academy they were both quiet from exhaustion. "That was a good private," Alexandra said, yawning.

"Yeah, Mr. Demidovski is awesome," Tristan agreed. They both looked across the street where someone seemed to be honking at them.

Alexandra shaded her eyes, trying to look at the car, and then her cell began to ring. She answered. "Is that idiot honking across from us you, Justin?" She sighed and put the phone back in her pocket. "You could probably get a ride with us," she offered.

"Yay."

"Stop saying yay, you sound like Taylor." They ran across the street, Alexandra getting in the front seat of the car next to her older brother. "Hey, Justin," she said, grinning. "Did you have fun in Whistler?"

"Hey, Justin," said Tristan, sticking his head between the two front seats. "How you doing, man?"

Justin shook his head and pulled out, nearly missing hitting a street performer. "Everyone sit in their own seats so I can breathe," he ordered.

Tristan sat back.

"I'm good, Tristan. It was fun, Lexi, except — I'll tell you about it later." Justin reached out and turned up the radio. Bruno Mars was singing about heartbreak. Justin suddenly turned the music down again. "Jesus. Okay, you know how I was dating Brooke?"

Alexandra nodded eagerly. "Yeah. Brooke. Dyed hair."

"She doesn't dye her hair!"

"Uh, yeah, she does," Alexandra and Tristan said together.

"Whatever. Doesn't even matter anymore because she dump — we broke up."

"Aw, Justin," said Alexandra, looking sympathetic. Her phone beeped with a text from Tristan, and she opened it.

"Your brother's hair looks really good."

Alexandra giggled.

"Are you guys laughing at me?" Justin asked, annoyed. "Geez, I know you don't give a shit about my life, Lexi, but you could at least pretend. I feel like crap." They giggled. Justin gave up and turned up the music. He drove Tristan home, threatening to drop them both off in Surrey every time they got too loud.

Once Alexandra and Justin got home, Alexandra hopped out of the car, going to head up to her room. "Lexi," Justin called after her.

"Yeah?" Alexandra asked, coming back.

"I went all the way downtown to pick you up even though I feel awful. Am I at least going to get a thank-you?"

"Thank you?" Alexandra said, her tone more rude than thankful.

"You know what? I don't even know why I bother. If it doesn't affect Alexandra Dunstan, it just isn't important, is it?" Justin stalked angrily up to his room, leaving behind a slightly confused and angry Alexandra.

Chapter Five

Julian Reese
Me — let's go dt for 4/20 after class! Tristan — what's 4/20? (facepalm).

"Julian."

Julian turned around. Theresa waved at him to come closer to her. He walked back, against the tide of his fellow dancers who were all exiting the studio, and to the corner where she was standing.

"Julian," she said quietly, her face bright with excitement. "I have asked your teachers for permission to coach you. And Taylor. I think she is a good partner for you."

Julian looked at her, confused. "You asked who? Um —"

"I asked the Demidovskis if I could coach you. And Taylor." Theresa enunciated each syllable and spoke slowly. "If you want, of course," she said suddenly. Julian realized that Theresa had not even considered the possibility that he — and Taylor — might not want to be coached by her.

"Do you mean — coaching for like, competition?"

"Yes," said Theresa. "Exactly. I feel that you need a mentor, Julian. A dancer is a gift. Each talent must be nurtured by someone who takes an interest. Do you understand me?"

"Uh, yeah." Julian said. "Um … thanks."

"It is no trouble at all." Theresa grabbed Julian by the shoulders and peered up at him earnestly. "Julian, you are very special. My impression of you is that you do not realize how special you are. You have talent, Julian, and I want to make sure you use that talent."

"Thank you."

"I don't like that I had to retire. I don't like teaching all these children. Most of them, they will never be dancers. It feels pointless, like there is no meaning to my life. But if I could coach you — and of course, Taylor — I think it would feel like I was making a difference. It would mean so much to me." She let go of him, and Julian stepped backwards.

He stared at her. "Thank you … I'll tell Taylor." He left for contemporary class.

"Julian!" Tristan called excitedly. He and Kageki were sitting on the studio floor, stretching. "Guess who's teaching today?"

Julian shrugged, walking over. "We have a different teacher?"

"Yeah, Kai called in sick! We have Leah today."

Julian's face lit up. "Really? That is so sweet. She's awesome." Julian had only gotten to take Leah's class once, and he still remembered it.

"Are you still wanting to get her to choreograph your

contemporary solo? Because you should totally ask her today. I'll ask her for you if you want."

"Yeah, Julian, you should," Kageki agreed. "She is so cool. Alexandra usually does stuff with her, and Alexandra is the best at contemporary."

"Um ..." Julian didn't know how to get out of this without telling them that he was choreographing his own stuff, and he *really* didn't want to tell them that.

Taylor walked up to them. "Are you talking about contemporary solos?!" she asked. "You should see what Julian's —"

"Taylor!" Julian said quickly. "I really wanted to talk to you about something. A secret?"

"What secret?" Tristan asked, curious.

"Nothing," said Julian, shaking his head. The others looked at him, confused.

"Oh!" Taylor exclaimed, covering her mouth with her hand. "Sorry, Julian, I get it."

"What?" Tristan asked annoyed. "Come on guys, this isn't fair."

"It's nothing, really," Julian assured him.

Tristan frowned, sulking, but he couldn't press Julian any further because suddenly Leah appeared in the doorway. Alexandra leaped up from her spot on the floor and ran to her, giving her a hug. Leah was a tall woman, and big: not fat, just large-boned and muscular. Her forehead had the sort of stretched-out look people get when they have been putting their hair in ponytails for too long, and her hair was dyed brown, but still had streaks left over from previous dye jobs. She wore a stretched out black pair of Lululemon pants, and a black T-shirt that said: I DANCE BECAUSE I WANT TO EXPLODE across it. Her eyeshadow was bronze and hastily applied, and her eyeliner was usually smeared due to her habit of yelling at her students, making herself sweat, and then wiping her face. Julian couldn't keep his grin off his face. She was just so cool.

Leah walked over to the CD player and set her bags down. "Who do I know?" she asked, looking around. "Alexandra, glad you're here. Tristan, are you going to be good today? Otherwise, get out." Jessica sat up straighter, waiting for Leah to recognize her, but she walked right by her. "Grace, of course." Leah nodded. "Anna? Where's Anna? Oh there you are. Remind me to talk to you after class — we need to change the time of your private. Kageki, of course, nice to see you again, *konnichiwa*. And —" Leah paused in front of Julian, frowning. "I know you," she protested, hitting her head with the palm of her hand. "Why?"

"I took your class once?" Julian said. "At Harbour Dance Centre."

"Hmm. The academy, right?" Leah stared at him, curious. "New kid."

"Uh, yes," Julian said, blushing. Everyone was staring at him.

Leah nodded and said hi to a few other students from other schools. "All right, everyone, let's get started. Spread out."

* * *

Julian leaped into the air and immediately fell to the ground, rolling out and up into a *penche*, his legs almost at 180 degrees. He was having so much fun in this contemporary class; it was nothing like how Sequoia taught them at the academy. Leah was letting them do a lot of improvization work, and the stuff that Leah had choreographed for them at the beginning of class was fun and left plenty of room for stylistic choices. To Julian, this class felt more natural than Sequoia's work, an extension of the technique he was learning at ballet class in a freer form. He hadn't once gotten yelled at for working in turn-out instead of parallel, and it felt great.

Leah stopped them, clapping her hands together in a rhythmic beat. Julian copied her, and Leah continued until she had the entire class clapping. She motioned for them to spread out into a circle. "Alexandra," she said, calling her to the centre of the circle. Alexandra nodded and took three steps into the circle before starting to improv dance to the tribal beats that were emanating from the corner. Leah had not approved of the idea that only ballet got live music, so she had brought in Cromwell Gilly, who was a drummer in his time away from designing. He worshipped the amount of money and freedom Leah gave him to design costumes for Movement Productions (and the amount of skin she let him show on her dancers) so he had no objection to occasionally drumming for free for her classes. Julian had never known that Cromwell drummed: he waved to him, trying to catch his eye.

"Julian."

Julian looked at Leah in surprise.

Leah motioned impatiently for him to enter the circle.

Julian walked in to the circle. He pretty much never got partnered with Alexandra. Usually she was paired with Tristan, or one of the Youth Company members that Mr. Yu occasionally coerced into attending *pas de deux* class. Even Jonathon sometimes got paired with Alexandra, but not Julian.

As he stepped forward, he suddenly felt nervous. It was one thing to improv and fool around with Taylor, another to do the same with Alexandra. She still made him a little nervous — she was so intense. He began to dance, remembering the corrections he had gotten from Kai that week: "Don't be afraid to use levels, remember to use as much space as you can. People can *see* the space you use, not just the lines you make." Julian stretched out his arms and gathered a huge ball of air, let it roll up his chest and knock him down, watched it dissipate, and then left it behind him.

"Julian," Leah called. "You have a partner. Use her!"

Julian turned around and gave a start of surprise, feeling a thrill of accomplishment as several students around him giggled. He stretched out his arms and ran swiftly toward her, intending to lift her up. Instead she ducked under his arm, rolled, and stepped into an *arabesque* away from him. Julian hesitated, unsure what to do. This wasn't how improv was supposed to work. You were supposed to follow your partner's lead. Alexandra began to *develope* and *ronds de jambe*, arching into a back bend. Julian saw her grin. *Well then. Fine.* He wasn't going to have Leah think he was bad at improv just because Alexandra wanted to show off. He began to dance close to her, weaving in and out, ducking his arms through hers, but completely ignoring her. He *grand battemented* his leg over her head without looking at her, making her wince. He saw her look at him, eyes black. She was angry now. Julian grinned.

"Very good!" Leah called. The drum beat began to change, getting quicker and harder to ignore. Cromwell began to sing in a language Julian didn't recognize as he drummed, and Julian and Alexandra moved faster, weaving in and out of each other now. Where improv was usually a game of keeping constant contact, they seemed to find themselves in a position of trying to dance as close as possible without touching.

"Sorry," Alexandra muttered, breaking the dance for a moment as she brushed a piece of her hair back after accidentally cutting Julian with a fingernail.

"No problem," Julian whispered back, narrowly avoiding kicking her in the stomach.

"You are allowed to touch each other," Leah called. She sounded like she was laughing, but Julian didn't turn around to check.

Julian reached out and hooked his elbow with Alexandra's, and they played with arm movement for a little while. Julian waited for an opening. He really wanted to impress Leah with one of the many lifts that Mr. Yu had been teaching him all year, but it didn't seem like Alexandra was going to give him the opening he needed to do that. Alexandra's arms floated upward as they danced, and Julian saw the free space at her waist. He reached out and lifted her, at an entirely awkward angle, and Alexandra seemed too surprised to do anything to help. She bent backwards and draped over his shoulder, and Julian kneeled on one leg so she could climb down, which she did. He grabbed her hand and they balanced their weight against each other, and then she ran back and he lifted her over his head. He grinned, proud of himself. At that moment, Alexandra shifted her back slightly, and Julian's left arm collapsed. After a full day of dancing he was too tired to support her anymore. Alexandra fell, Julian slid beneath her, they both ended up in a pile of limbs staring at each other, confused, as the rest of the class laughed and/or ran over to make sure they were all right.

"You dropped me," Alexandra said accusingly. "Ow."

"Sorry," Julian said sincerely. "Your back moved."

"Is anything broken?" Leah asked, giving them both a hand up. "No? Okay then. That was an entirely unnecessary show-off move back there, but the beginning was good. You guys look good together." She moved off to the front to begin teaching them the next part to a dance they were all learning, and Alexandra followed her to the front line. Julian stayed in the back line where he could copy the choreography from everyone else (he was still rather slow at picking up choreography). *That was fun*, he thought. Alexandra was an awesome dancer, too bad she didn't seem to like him. She never spoke to him, even when they were sitting in the same group. *Besides*, he reminded himself, *she and Tristan like dancing with each other. But Leah said we look good dancing together ...*

He watched Taylor try to move to the front and get firmly blocked by Tristan, Alexandra, and Anna. She ended up in the middle line, and having spent more time trying to get in the front line than learning the exercise, she flailed around doing most of it wrong and that which she did right was two counts behind the rest of the class.

Leah shook her head as she watched her. "Blondie!" she called from the front. "Learn the combination before you kill someone." Taylor nodded and worked behind Alexandra, copying her every move with a one-count delay.

Julian sighed. Taylor was at his level, not Alexandra. He turned his attention back to the exercise and began to focus, trying to make his body move with the sharpness that Kageki danced with instead of the limpness that Julian usually saw reflected back to him in the mirror.

"Good job, Julian!" Leah called out. "Make it sharper! Be fierce!" Julian smiled, and worked even harder. Spring Seminar was turning out to be so much fun.

After class, Julian got changed fast and then dawdled behind, fooling around with his cellphone on a bench in the lobby as the other dancers left. "Want a ride, Jules?" Taylor asked, hovering near the door. She adjusted her oversized baseball cap nervously, and Julian thought to himself that she looked like a ten-year-old trying to look like Avril Lavigne.

"No, I'm good," Julian assured her.

Alexandra and Tristan walked by, Tristan with his arm on Alexandra's shoulder as they talked about something so quietly that Julian could not hear. "Bye, Jules," Tristan said over his shoulder as Alexandra continued to talk, her flow uninterrupted.

"Bye." Julian walked back and forth on the lobby floor, backwards, then forwards, pivoting faster on the ball of his foot each time he switched direction. He had just almost started to do the Charleston, when he saw Leah get out of the elevator.

Julian quickly leaned on the wall, and began to type on his phone as if that was why he was still there. Leah walked toward him and then through the door, Cromwell Gilly walking behind her carrying his drums. Julian put his phone in his jacket pocket and swung up to a stand, following them out the door.

"Hey." Leah turned around, seeing Julian walking behind them. "Good work today, Julian."

"Thanks." Julian felt himself blush.

"No, really. You're going to be good in a few years. Don't underestimate yourself. To be honest, I think your biggest obstacle is lack of confidence."

Julian frowned. He had never thought of himself as lacking in confidence. He knew he screwed stuff over for himself, but that was usually just a lack of work put in, or him psyching himself out. "Thanks."

"Don't say thanks, work on it."

Julian nodded. He looked at Cromwell Gilly's arm full of drums. "Want some help with that? You aren't bussing, are you?"

"No, I'm giving him a ride," Leah answered for him.

"But if you could help me bring this stuff to the car, I'd appreciate it," Cromwell Gilly said hurriedly.

Julian took half of Cromwell Gilly's armful and began to walk with them to the car, finding himself walking between them. "Where are you from, Julian?" Leah asked.

"The Island."

"Where on the Island?"

"Valdez. It's not on Vancouver Island, it's one of the Gulf Islands — it's reeeeaaally small, you've probably never heard of it."

"No, I've heard of it." Leah pushed a button and her trunk popped open. Cromwell and Julian began to load the drums in the trunk. "So, where do you live here?" Leah asked.

"I homestay. With Mr. Yu. Do you know him?"

"Yes, of course." Cromwell closed the trunk. Leah stepped around to the side of the car, and paused, digging around in her pockets for her keys. "Do you want a ride home?"

"It's sort of far …"

"I know where he lives, Julian. Come on, get in."

Julian got in, moving aside a box of CDs, and putting it on top of a child's car seat. "You do?" He closed the car door behind him as Cromwell joined Leah in the front.

She began to pull out, peering backwards through the pile of drums in the backseat. "I used to go to the academy."

Julian's mouth fell open. "What? Really?"

"Yes."

"But — you — I mean, I thought you were all contemporary."

"Things change, Julian."

"Yeah."

"You know, that's what I hate about the academy," Leah said as she turned onto Granville Street Bridge. "They teach you all to be perfect little ballet students, and then you think you are a failure if that doesn't happen. Look at me, I didn't become a ballet dancer, and I'm fine." Julian looked at her hands, white from the strength of her grip on the steering wheel.

Yeah, you seem fine — not. "I guess, yeah. But, don't you sort of have to think like that to be driven enough to become a ballet dancer? Like, if you want to do other stuff, too, you probably don't like ballet enough."

Leah stared through the window. "Julian, I have seen so many dancers go through that school, and yes, you are right — the ones that are really good, they do have that kind of insane focus, that kind of drive. But what about the ones that aren't like that? That might be good at something else, or better at contemporary? They come out of ballet, and they're brainwashed into thinking that they are a failure if they don't become a ballet dancer."

"Well, yeah," said Julian. "But technically, they are a failure then, aren't they? If they wanted to be a ballet dancer and then they aren't?"

Leah spun the wheel, heading up and east toward Mr. Yu's house. "No. They're not. I blame the academy for teaching you that."

Julian decided it was in his best interests to drop the subject since Leah was driving him home and was his teacher. But she was wrong. He sat back in his seat. Beside Leah, Cromwell Gilly turned around and winked at Julian.

"I saw that," Leah said dryly. "I know you all think I'm this crazy old woman who's always on your case, but I'm right. I'm always right."

"Okay," said Julian, laughing. He smiled as he stared out the window. It was so nice being driven home instead of taking the bus, his legs and back and arms and — okay, his whole body — ached. The combination of having ballet and contemporary class every day was giving him whole new muscles. The sun was beginning to set, and from the high street they were driving on he could see the streets below, all the cheap matched-set houses, gleaming in the orange light. "Cromwell Gilly," Julian asked sleepily. "How come you like to be called by your full name? And is that your real name?"

"No," said Cromwell Gilly dryly, "It is not my real name. But it will be my name. Someday you are going to pick up this perfect black jacket, and look in the inside tag, and it is going to say Cromwell Gilly. And then you are going to have to put it down, because you will be a ballet dancer so you will be far too poor to buy it, and I hope you aren't a thief."

"Oh." Julian nodded. "Cool." Leah pulled to a stop in front of the Yu's house, and Julian climbed out. "Thanks, Leah," he said.

"No problem." Leah pulled off in a hurry, her old car making a screeching noise as she pulled away, racing along the quiet street.

Julian walked around the back of his homestay and went in through the back of the house, being careful not to set off any of the alarms. The Yus had two separate alarms, one for the downstairs where their homestay students stayed, and one for the upstairs where they lived. The downstairs kitchen was dark, and Julian didn't bother turning on the light, walking through and on to his room. He flung his bag down on the floor and lay down on the bed on his back. A heavy, furry shape crawled up and lay on his chest, digging its claws into Julian's chest. "Hey, Tigger," Julian said, petting Mrs. Yu's large over-fed cat. Tigger purred. "Tigger," said Julian, sitting him up and moving his paws, "would you make me really good please? Magically? I need to get stronger, and I need to get more flexible, and my musicality sucks, and my *pirouettes* aren't as good as Kageki's, and my jumps aren't as clean as Tristan's." Tigger just purred, and Julian sighed, laying his head back down on the bed. He closed his eyes: he just wanted to lie there, for a minute …

"Julian!" Mao said in his ear.

Julian sat up suddenly, disoriented. "What? Huh?"

"Dinnertime."

"Oh, yeah, okay, yeah …" Julian rubbed his eyes and stumbled out to the dining room where they always ate.

Leon, Keiko, and Mr. and Mrs. Yu were already sitting there. Mao and Julian sat down, Julian taking his usual seat in between Mao and Keiko and leaving Leon to talk to Mr. Yu. To his surprise, Mr. Yu suddenly spoke to him.

"Julie. How is Spring Seminar going?"

"Good," said Julian. "It's — really fun."

"Good. You going to win something?"

"Um, I don't know."

"Should win something. Work harder, uh?"

"Yes," Julian agreed. He reached out and began to fill his plate with white rice and stir-fry. "Um, Mr. Yu, I have a question …"

"Yes?" Mr. Yu lowered his eyebrows, frowning.

"Today we had Leah for contemporary, and she said she used to go to the academy."

"Hm. Yes. I remember, she did. You ask her to do a contemporary solo for you?"

Julian shrugged. "Maybe," he lied. He began to eat his dinner, Mao and Keiko watching him, ready to correct his use of chopsticks. He thought he was getting better, they felt that he still needed much improvement. He accidentally sprayed a piece of chicken into Keiko's hair. "Oh, sorry …"

"Use fork!" Mr. Yu demanded from the other side of the table. Julian kept using his chopsticks and pretended he didn't hear.

Chapter Six

Kaitlyn Wardle
Everybody come and see the Spring Seminar show today!

Kaitlyn stood in the front line of her group, on the black floor of the small stage in Scotiabank Dance Centre. The stage was not raised from the ground, and the curtains were not drawn to form wings on the stage, so it was hard for Kaitlyn to feel like it was a proper performance. In any case, it wasn't really, it was just so the parents and the teachers who wished to attend and the ballet society members could all see what the students had been working on during Spring Break. Kaitlyn looked up: she could see Taylor's mother up in the middle sitting with Chloe's mother, and over in the corner was Grace's mother and Anna's dad, and there were Tristan's parents, and down, right in the front and middle, was her mother. Cecelia was sitting cross-legged, moving her foot back and forth. She saw Kaitlyn watching her and mouthed: "Smile!" Kaitlyn obeyed. Cecelia patted her stomach, and Kaitlyn sucked her stomach in farther.

Theresa and Leah walked out, and everyone started to clap. Beside Kaitlyn, Taylor whispered, "I just want to know who's going to get something! I'm so nervous — my mom really wants me to get something."

"Mmm," said Kaitlyn. "You should probably be quiet." In the audience, Cecelia frowned at her to not talk.

"I just really hate waiting," Taylor whispered, fidgeting. "I wish they would just tell us, and *then* they could like talk." She looked at the podium and sighed: the board was still going through their annual meeting. "What are minutes, anyway?" Taylor asked.

"Taylor …" Kaitlyn whispered back.

"What? I'm not good at school, okay?"

Kaitlyn didn't answer her; she didn't know what minutes were, either. Finally they called Theresa and Leah up on stage to hand out the awards. Cecelia glared at Kaitlyn. "What?" Kaitlyn mouthed back at her. Cecelia pointed at her mouth, and Kaitlyn quickly began smiling again.

Leah stood up first to give out her awards. "I am afraid their original teacher, Kai, is still ill," she explained. "But it has been my pleasure to teach these dancers this week. Each and every one of them is extremely talented. Now, let me call out some names for the awards which the Vancouver Ballet Society has so generously provided — Alexandra …" she said, smiling.

Alexandra got the biggest amount of money, Chloe Song and Michael Grant in the younger class both received a prize, Tristan and Julian each got something, Anna got a rather big scholarship, and a few dancers who didn't go to the academy got bursaries, and then Leah was finished. Kaitlyn didn't get anything. *But it's okay, it's just contemporary*, she told herself. She smiled harder, waiting. Beside her, she could feel Taylor fidgeting nervously.

Theresa stepped up to the podium next, smiling. She gave Leah a hug, and then took the small microphone. "It has been such a pleasure teaching these students," she said brightly. "I don't know if they told you, but they have been my little guinea pigs! They've been amazing these few weeks, thank you for loaning them to me." The audience clapped loudly. "Now to reward some of these students for their extraordinary work." Theresa started from thc smallest bursaries and moved upwards; Jessica got something, and Anna, who grabbed her rose and envelope with a dazzling smile and hugged Theresa, making everyone laugh; and Chloe and Michael each got something, and Grace. Kaitlyn waited patiently for the bigger, more important awards to be called.

"Kaitlyn Wardle." Kaitlyn looked up, surprised. "Yes, you, dear," Theresa said, laughing. Kaitlyn walked over, trying to look happy. *Maybe this doesn't mean I didn't get a big award*, she told herself quickly. *Maybe they're going to give me two*. Kaitlyn took the rose and envelope from Theresa and curtseyed politely. She walked to the line of dancers who had already gotten awards and waited to hear her name called again.

"Alexandra Dunstan," Theresa called, and Alexandra walked down and received her award. She and Theresa smiled politely at each other. Kaitlyn couldn't decide if Theresa liked Alexandra or not. She corrected her a lot, but she didn't seem to like her.

"Tristan Patel." Tristan walked confidently across the stage to get his award, and gave Theresa a hug. Kaitlyn rolled her eyes. He was so obviously just copying Anna.

"Taylor Audley." Kaitlyn watched, horrified, as Taylor practically bounced across the stage to get her award, a huge grin on her face. Kaitlyn looked at Cecelia. *Oh no.* To Kaitlyn's horror, her mother appeared to be crying. The audience was hard to see from under the bright stage lights, but she could see her mother clearly in the front row as she was illuminated in the lights, and there were definitely tears running down her face. Kaitlyn quickly looked away, staring at Theresa. She crossed her fingers. *Please, please, let me get what I want ...*

"And then, last, but certainly not least, Julian Reese!" Julian looked up. He had obviously been drifting off and not paying attention. He practically ran across the stage and awkwardly took his envelope and rose, looking more embarrassed than happy about his award. He shifted his envelope and rose to one hand, and ran his other hand through his hair. Theresa reached out a small, but strong hand and hooked her arm around his shoulder, pulling him in close to her. Julian was taken off guard and nearly fell over.

Kaitlyn looked over at her mother: she was still crying.

"This young man," said Theresa, "is an excellent example of what this generation has to offer. He has so much talent, and I have not once seen him give less than 100 percent. Julian, there is no doubt in my mind that you deserve this scholarship." Theresa wrapped her arms around him and hugged him. Julian tried to pull away, but she hugged him tighter. Finally she let him go, and he stepped away, his rose losing petals on the stage. One of the Vancouver Ballet Society ladies took over the podium, and that was it, the awards were over, and it was time go to the potluck.

Kaitlyn followed her mother out of the theatre, her *pointe* shoes making a clapping noise on the floor as she tried to keep up. Cecelia stopped in the hall. "I can't believe this!" she said loudly, tears pouring down her middle-aged face.

"Mom!" Kaitlyn hissed, looking around. She could see several mothers and students around who weren't from the academy. "There's a bathroom."

Cecelia followed her into the bathroom. "Kaitlyn, what happened?" she asked, grabbing toilet paper and wiping her face. "Why didn't you tell me that Theresa hated you? I would have done something about it, I would have talked to someone, I would have *done* something!"

"Mom! I don't think Theresa hates me —"

"What are you talking about?! Of course she hates you, she gave you the same amount of money as Jessica! *Jessica!* And of course she likes Taylor better than you, that woman is a psycho. She clearly chose based on body type. What were you doing in class all week? Were you smiling? That woman is clearly off her rocker. And giving a scholarship to Taylor ahead of you — did she *see* Taylor's chest? Her breasts are going to be as big as her mother's. She's never going to get a job as a ballet dancer!"

"Mom!" Kaitlyn said, louder. A younger kid opened the door, and then quickly left again. "Please don't say *breasts*. Theresa doesn't hate me, I don't think, okay? Can you please just stop it?"

"Don't you dare use that tone with me. I don't want you going out there. Come on, I'll drive you to your private."

Kaitlyn wavered. She didn't really want to leave right now; yeah, she was embarrassed about not winning, but she wanted to go to the potluck. Besides, it would look like she had left because she hadn't won if she left right away. "I have to go out. I — I told Taylor I would be right back."

"Kaitlyn. We're leaving. Right now." Kaitlyn followed Cecelia out of the bathroom, sulking, and went to go get her stuff.

The car was right where Mrs. Wardle had left it, parked beside apartment buildings on the west side of the Dance Centre. Kaitlyn climbed in the front, sitting beside Mrs. Wardle, and folded her arms. "I don't know what *you* have to be mad about," Mrs. Wardle snapped. "You didn't have to sit and watch your daughter lose because she couldn't stop stuffing her fat face."

Kaitlyn glared out the window and wiped her eyes. "I hate you."

"You could have won everything," Mrs. Wardle said, ignoring her. "You are a million times more talented than anyone in that room. You are almost fifteen years old now. You need to get your priorities in order."

"I did work!" Kaitlyn exploded. "Okay? I don't know what happened, Theresa just doesn't like me."

"That woman is a disgusting psycho," Mrs. Wardle stated. "I can't believe that you didn't warn me about this earlier! Kaitlyn, even *Angela* is skinnier than you."

Kaitlyn sat back in her chair, confused. "What?" She didn't even consider Angela competition. At five-foot-nothing with a soft body, a too-large head, and short legs, Angela was nobody's idea of a ballet dancer. In fact, Kaitlyn didn't even think she was doing festival at all.

"You need to work harder. You need to get your focus back. Concentrate on you, ignore everything else."

Kaitlyn nodded.

"Don't just nod at me! I'm serious. You have been all over the place this year. Do you know what this is going to *do* to your reputation? What do you think everyone is going to say about this, Kaitlyn? You haven't lost *anything* before! I remember when you were three and you won first for that piece, the one where you were the little girl at a party, in that purple dress, do you remember?"

"Yeah."

"You haven't gotten anything but first since! Do you have any idea how fast everyone is going to know that you lost today?"

"I know! I'm sorry, okay?"

"Well, fix it. Get in that studio and start working. Show them what you can do. Don't worry about trying to make friends with these people. They'll be friends with you if you are better than them."

"I know!"

"Kaitlyn, I mean it. If you don't start getting better, what are you going to do? You've already lost Swanhilda and this, what more do you have to lose before you decide to work?"

"Mom! Stop it."

Cecelia wiped her eyes. "I just don't know what to do anymore. Do you remember when you were young? You were so cute, and so skinny — that is who you are. You have to get that back."

"I know."

"Today is a new beginning, okay?"

"Fine."

Mrs. Wardle pulled up in front of the academy. "Good luck."

"Bye," Kaitlyn mumbled, getting out of the car.

"Kaitlyn?"

"Yeah?"

"I love you, sweetie."

Kaitlyn turned and left, walking toward the studio. She looked at her cellphone — she had fifteen minutes to get changed and warmed up for her first private with Mr. Moretti. *I hate her. I wonder how many people saw her crying today? Why couldn't I have just gotten that scholarship?*

Kaitlyn quickly got changed and then started to put on her *pointe* shoes. She tied her ribbons, tucked them in, and then stood up, rolling up and down to try and warm her feet. She felt her left foot crack and breathed a sigh of relief. One more — and yes, her right foot cracked, too. She slid into the splits and briefly did them all three ways before standing up and cracking her back. She looked up at the large clock in the academy's lobby. One minute. She grabbed her bag and went into the studio where her private had been scheduled. The studio was still empty, Mr. Moretti wasn't there yet. Kaitlyn stood at the side for a moment, basking in the feeling of having the large airy studio all to herself instead of being one of many sweaty bodies taking class in it. She walked over to the CD player and put her disc in, getting it set up, and then walked to the centre of the studio. She grinned and prepared; *"Ichi, ni, san!"* she counted herself off in Japanese. And then she was turning. She started off with a triple *pirouette*, and then began to *fouette,* doing a single *fouette*, then a double, repeating the pattern. She managed to continue the pattern for a full set of thirty-two, and then landed with a hop at the last second.

She grinned at her own reflection in the mirror. She couldn't wait until she was a principal with a ballet company and could do the black swan coda for real. Of course, she would be skinnier then. She glanced at the clock: Mr. Moretti should have been there already, it was seven minutes past. She went to the CD player and turned it on, beginning to run through her variation. She had decided that she wanted to do *Grande Pas Classique.* It had lots of turns, she liked it, and she knew that there was a beautiful tutu in the academy's costume room that she could rent for it. After she had run through her variation once, she looked up at the clock. Ten minutes past. Had he forgotten he was scheduled to coach her today?

Grace walked in, and paused, surprised. "Oh, sorry. Do you have a private here?"

"Uh, yeah," Kaitlyn said. "It says so on the schedule."

"Oh. I didn't hear anything, so I thought it was just you practicing. Who's coaching you?"

"Mr. Moretti."

"He's not here yet?"

"No."

Grace looked up at the clock. It was twelve minutes past. "Well, mind if I rehearse in here until he gets here?" Without waiting for an answer, she set her bag at the side and walked over to the CD player, changing the music to her own. In a moment the sound of Swanhilda's first act variation from *Coppelia* started playing. Kaitlyn frowned, watching Grace run through the variation.

"Are you doing that for competition?" Kaitlyn asked as Grace finished.

"No," Grace said, smiling. "This is for a presentation. Mr. Demidovski wants me to dance it for the Russian ambassadors when they come to visit the school."

Kaitlyn bit her lip. If Mr. Demidovski had gotten Grace to do this solo for the presentation, it sort of sounded like he had already given her the part of Swanhilda in the academy's production of *Coppelia* for June. Which meant it would be even more difficult to get her role back. She looked at the clock; it was fifteen minutes past now. Where was Mr. Moretti? She went into the hall and into the office, leaning on Gabriel's desk as she waited for him to notice her. "What can I do for you, Kaitlyn?" Gabriel asked, turning around and smiling after he had shifted his papers for long enough to realize that she was not going away.

"I'm supposed to have a private with Mr. Moretti," Kaitlyn explained. "But he's not there, so I was wondering if maybe he called in sick or something."

Gabriel shoved his glasses back as he thought, sitting his large Norwegian body back in the small chair. "No, no, I don't think so," he assured her. He picked up a bag of yogurt-covered raisins that were sitting beside him. "Want some?" Kaitlyn shrugged and took two out of the bag, popping one in her mouth. Gabriel leaned toward her to whisper, "They are Mrs. Demidovski's." Kaitlyn's eyes widened, and she felt like spitting the raisin out.

"Won't she mind?" she asked.

"No. Not if we don't tell her," Gabriel assured her.

They both turned around as they heard the main entrance door close with a bang, and muffled curses in Italian. Kaitlyn shoved the raisin back in the bag and passed it back to Gabriel, but it was too late, Mr. Moretti had turned the corner and was peering in the office, his tall frame almost completely covered in a green tarp-like poncho that sprayed water all over the walls and floor every time he moved. "What are you doing?"

"Uh." Kaitlyn's mind went blank. "I was just checking with Gabriel that — um —"

"You should be in the studio rehearsing!" Mr. Moretti said angrily. "What, I am not here, so you don't need to practise? It is not for me that you become a ballet dancer, it is for you. If you manage, which is highly doubtful." He strode over to the studio and wrenched open the door. Inside Grace was still practising, and she ignored them. "See? This is what a good student does. Now go, warm-up — I cannot coach you cold like this."

Kaitlyn walked into the studio as Mr. Moretti went into the office to complain about his last paycheque.

Grace looked over at her, and Kaitlyn felt the scorn she felt for herself reflected in Grace's eyes. She looked at the ground and began to stretch, her cheeks red.

At half-past, Mr. Moretti finally showed up, and Grace quietly exited. Mr. Moretti didn't bother to say anything to Kaitlyn, instead walking over to the front of the room and setting his stuff down. He pulled off his grey sweatshirt that said VIBA Nutcracker 2011 on the back, and set it on the chair.

Kaitlyn waited, nervously shifting. She had stopped rehearsing when he came in. As he tuned to look at her, she began to practice her triple *pirouette en dehors.* Mr. Moretti cracked his back idly as he watched her. "You are frightfully lazy baby, aren't you?"

Kaitlyn smiled, not sure how to respond.

Mr. Moretti walked over and put his hand on Kaitlyn's forehead. "No fever. Just lazy." He walked back and leaned on the mirror. "All right. Let us see how big of a mess this is, yes? Begin." He pushed Play on the remote control.

As Kaitlyn finished her solo, she fought to breathe. The studio was starting to heat up with her sweat already.

"Are you pregnant?" Mr. Moretti asked as she held her closing position.

"No."

"Well, it looks it. If you are not the old fat Grandma, you should not look it." He walked over to her, poked her in the stomach with one finger, and ran another up her spine to make it lengthen. "Like this."

He bent his head down to hers and looked in the mirror, stretching out her arm and then his, comparing the two. "Your *port de bras*, it is like ice. Blocks of ice moving through space. It is so ugly, even in *Titanic* they did not show such lumps. Look at my arm, it is beautiful. If the old grandpa can do it, you can. Do it once more, just the arms. Bend." In one swift motion, he grabbed both of her arms by the wrist, causing them to hang down. "Look," he commanded, pointing in the mirror.

Kaitlyn stared at the mirror. She was bent forward, and her arms flopped in front like a doll in the *Nutcracker* that has not come alive yet. On her back she could only see muscle and her spine: all of her little bones were covered by smooth skin.

"Soft," Mr. Moretti said, disgusted.

Kaitlyn nodded and quickly stood up.

"From the beginning. Just the arms. No legs." Kaitlyn ran back to the corner and waited. Mr. Moretti's finger hovered over the button on the CD player. "Actually," he said, turning around, "I don't think this variation is quite the thing for you, baby."

Kaitlyn stared at him. This variation was perfect for her, it was a largely technical variation, and she could smile her way through it. She'd already been rehearsing it, too; there wasn't enough time before competition for her to change.

"I think," said Mr. Moretti, looking through the index on the back of a variation CD that had been left in the studio, "that we can find something a little bit more suitable. Something that will challenge you. Make you grow." He stopped, having found something. "Why not *Flames of Paris*?"

Kaitlyn opened her mouth and then closed it again. There was no way she was going to win with that variation! "Okay …"

Mr. Moretti turned to show her the version he wanted her to do, and behind him Kaitlyn obediently learned the steps. *It's okay*, she told herself. It's just one private. *My mom can explain to him that I wanted to do the other variation later.*

Chapter Seven

Taylor Smaylor Audley
So exited to perform at the asembly tom!! And nervus :p :0 :D

Taylor lay her head on her desk, trying not to attract her teacher's attention. It was futile. "Taylor? Ms. Audley?" Mrs. Flowers called. "What do you think?"

Taylor sat up and stared at her blankly. "Um — I think that — you know, that the watersheds are — well, we need water, and, like, they make us have water, so that's good and people shouldn't make it dirty, right?"

Mrs. Cowley nodded like Taylor had just said something terribly insightful and turned back to the slides she was showing the class. Technically since they were in grade nine, they should have been learning about the medieval age, not watersheds, but Mrs. Flowers was the Environment Club's sponsor and she wanted to make sure that they knew enough about the environment that they would at least think about helping out. Taylor turned over her BlackBerry on her knee and checked it.

"Taylor, I hope I don't see you doing what I think you're doing," Mrs. Flowers called. Taylor sighed and put the phone back.

"I'm not doing anything," she told Mrs. Flowers, putting both of her hands back on the table.

After class, Taylor got up first to leave. Mrs. Flowers stopped her. "Taylor, are you doing okay?" she asked, as the last of the students left the classroom.

"Um, yeah, why?" Taylor asked. She felt put on the spot, and didn't appreciate it.

"Well, to be honest, you haven't been putting the work in that you could for your assignments, and I was wondering if there was anything you wanted to talk about."

"No, everything's good. Just busy with dance."

"Right. Well, if you ever need anyone to talk to —"

"Thanks, Mrs. Flowers."

"Well. You can go then — I look forward to seeing your performance at the assembly today!"

"Thanks!" Taylor left the room, seeing Kaitlyn and Jessica out in the hall. They began to walk downstairs.

"What'd she want?" Kaitlyn asked curiously.

"Oh, she just thought that I looked like something was wrong or something," Taylor brushed it off. "You know what teachers are like."

"Yeah," Jessica agreed. "Like, you know Ms. Bueller, the English teacher? She was always annoying me last year, about did I need counselling for my problems?"

Taylor looked at Kaitlyn, and they both started to giggle: Jessica definitely did need help for her problems.

"It's all because of that stupid nurse who gave us shots," Jessica said, frowning. "I'll go around calling *her* anorexic. Except she was really fat."

The bell for second class rang. "I have to go get ready!" Taylor exclaimed.

"For sure, good luck," Kaitlyn said. Taylor gave them both a hug and made her way to the downstairs washroom.

The halls emptied as everyone else went to their class, and the washroom was soon empty. Taylor got changed into her contemporary outfit and put on some more makeup, eyeliner, a bit of blush, and some lipstick. *Stupid bathroom lights* ... There wasn't a single bathroom in McKinley that had good lighting. Taylor reached in her bag and patted around: there, she did have her CD. She left, going to the theatre to warm up and look at the stage.

The lights were already on, and she could hear laughter above her. *The tech club must already be up there*, she thought. She stepped onto the stage, and a teacher she didn't recognize stopped her. "Taylor Audley?"

"Yeah."

"Okay — dancing, right?"

"Yup." Taylor looked behind him, at the wings. There were a couple rhythmic gymnasts, a small boy she thought might be a pianist, and a girl who she knew was an opera singer. "Do you want my CD?"

"Sure. Actually, could you please take it up to the students up there?" He pointed overhead to the tech booth.

"Sure." Taylor began walking in the direction he had pointed, and ended up in front of a partially closed door with laughter emanating from it. She knocked, and there was sudden silence and then a burst of giggling. Taylor backed away from the door.

"Who goeth there?" a boy asked in goofy accent.

"Me," Taylor called back.

"That is very descriptive, Me," the voice remarked. "Have we perchance met before?" The boy opened the door and looked at her. He was very skinny and pale. He opened the door a little farther to show off the rest of the occupants of the room, who were all staring at her. Taylor suddenly wished she wasn't just wearing her costume with a Lululemon jacket over top.

"The teacher down there said to give my CD to you guys," she explained.

"Awesomola, my Sharona," he answered, staring at her. "Do you go to our school?"

A snort came from a red-haired girl sitting on a chair in the back doing something odd with a Buffy the Vampire Slayer doll.

"Uh, yeah I do," Taylor answered. "But I'm in the Super Achievers program." She handed him a CD and started to leave. Behind her she could hear a discussion.

"All the Super Achievers girls are bitches, Zack," a voice said.

She could hear Matt answer: "Dude. Emily was not every Special Achievers girl. She wasn't even a representative example." Taylor heard a crash and a stream of creative expletives. She walked slowly, waiting to see if they were going to say anything more about her, but they appeared to be busy dealing with the results of the crash.

Taylor bobbed up and down in the wings, both nervous and excited. She could hear the students in the audience, closer than a regular theatre and louder. She'd found that she had to do her solo with bare feet instead of *pointe* shoes because the floor of the stage was not made for *pointe* work, to say the least. It was so slippery that Taylor had almost put rosin on her bare feet before deciding not to experiment. She could hear the principal, Mr. Grant, talking at great length about how McKinley Secondary School was a much better school than any other school in Vancouver, and how Super Achievers was one of the reasons why McKinley was so much better.

"And the next talented McKinley student I have great pleasure in presenting," she heard Mr. Grant say; "is a grade nine in intensive dance training at the Vancouver International Ballet academy. Taylor Audley, performing her contemporary piece 'All I Ever Wanted.' Let's hear a round of applause for Taylor, everyone."

Taylor heard her music began to play, and winced. She was supposed to start on. Her CD had been labelled with 'Starts on.' Why were they doing this to her? "Starts on" meant that they were supposed to start the music once she was on the stage and ready, not still waiting in the wings. Had they even bothered to look at the CD?

"Just a moment everybody," she could hear Mr. Grant say into the microphone as the music turned off.

A teacher came up to Taylor, and she quickly explained what was wrong.

"Let's try again, everybody. Taylor Audley."

Taylor took a breath, and then walked on, slowly, confidently, trying to take her time. She'd told everyone that she'd gotten a contemporary teacher outside of the academy to do her solo, but in truth Julian had choreographed it. She'd promised him that she'd do his choreography if she liked it, and she *really* liked this solo. He'd originally choreographed it for himself, but it worked well as a girl's solo, too. Taylor looked out into the audience and saw Julian sitting with Tristan and Alexandra in the second row. Julian was sitting forward, twisting his hands nervously on his lap like somehow it was him about to go on stage, not Taylor. Which in a way was true, but only Julian and Taylor knew that. She met his eyes, trying to tell him that it was all good. The music began to play, and Taylor forgot about Julian, about herself, about not messing up, and began to dance.

It was odd dancing on this stage. Taylor felt almost like she was dancing in the studio, everyone was so close. The lights were blinding, though; she didn't know what the tech club thought they were doing. As she *chained* in diagonal, she noticed that there was a spotlight following her. She stepped into a *penche,* kicked herself into a handstand, rolled out into a dramatic huddle of pain, flicked up in a sudden motion, and ran into one of the highest *jetés* she had ever done on stage.

"Whoot!" she heard someone call from the audience, and she would have grinned if the dance hadn't been tragic. Instead she channelled that energy into her grand *pirouette*, turning in attitude, *chaine*, *chaine*, and then a *coupe jeté en tourne* to fall to the ground and up. She felt as if her solo were over too fast, but she could hear the applause as she stood up to take a bow and now she let herself grin. They had liked it; a high school audience was not the sort to fake enthusiasm, at least for a grade nine girl who was unknown to most. She ran off the stage and almost ran into Zack. "Hey," he said, grinning. "Did you like the spotlight?"

Taylor shook her head, giggling. "You guys are nuts." She started to run off: she'd have to hurry to get to the academy on time.

"But, the right kind of nuts, right?" Zack called after her.

Taylor got changed into her jeans and shirt, pulled on her shiny new Vans and walked over to the mirror, rubbing off the blush and some of the lipstick. Not all of the lipstick would come off, so she put some pale pink lip gloss over top to cover it up, and then she slung her bag over her shoulder. Her counsellor was outside the door, and Taylor frowned, surprised. "Hi, Mr. Briggs," she said politely.

"Hi, Taylor," Mr. Briggs said, smiling at her. He seemed to have something on his mind, and Taylor ran through what she had done lately, getting worried. "Excellent job today. You really make us proud."

"Thanks." Taylor shifted her feet, confused.

"Do you mind if I talk to you in my office for a moment?" Mr. Briggs asked.

"Um, yeah. Sure," Taylor agreed. They walked to the counselling suite in almost silence. Taylor didn't mind. Even though she was worried about what Mr. Briggs wanted to say to her, she always found his presence very soothing. He was that sort of person. He didn't tell you what to do, he just placed information in your hands in such a way that you came to the right conclusion by yourself and then he praised you for your admirable grasp of life.

Mr. Briggs opened the door and let Taylor in. "After you. Have a seat."

Taylor set down her backpack and sat in the comfortable armchair Mr. Briggs kept in his office. Mr. Briggs sat down at his desk and pulled up her student profile on his computer screen. "How are your classes going, Taylor?" he asked absently as he did this.

"Good, good," Taylor said, feeling herself about to babble. "I mean, I'm doing okay, but not great —"

"You've been working hard at dance, though?" Mr. Briggs looked at her.

"Yes," Taylor said, suddenly reminded of the fact that she had skipped contemporary class the other day because her ankle had been hurting and she hadn't wanted to watch at the side.

"Good then. Now, Taylor, I called you in here because as you know, the Super Achievers program requires a B+ average, yes?"

"Yeah?" Taylor giggled nervously. She hadn't had a B+ average since grade two when her mother had bought her teacher a fruit-dehydrating machine. She assumed that the B+ average requirement at McKinley was just one of those things that wasn't a real rule.

"Now, I just want you to take a look over here —" Mr. Briggs swivelled his chair around to look at his computer, and Taylor stood up to peer over his shoulder.

Taylor's grades appeared on the screen next to her school photo. She looked at her photo: she had worn her yellow tank top and straightened her hair, and the blond and yellow looked really good with her blue eyes and the mottled blue-grey photo background. She didn't remember where she had put that necklace, though — it was a silver chain with a heart pendant in it that her aunt had given to her. She'd better find it before her aunt came to visit again …

"Taylor, look here," said Mr. Briggs, pointing at her grades, "do you see a problem?" He adjusted his glasses and pointed at the first class. "Social Studies. 19 percent."

Taylor nodded, trying to focus. "I might do better after our project?" she tried.

"Math. You're getting seventeen percent here."

"I'm going to just retake it online or something."

"English. Twenty-nine percent."

"I forgot to hand a story in. I'll give it to her reeeee-aaaalllly soon."

"Science. It says here that Mr. Barrie wants to talk to you before gives you an interim mark."

"Yeah — um, he thinks I was cheating on a test. But it totally wasn't my fault, this guy, Brandon? He was whispering all the answers to me, but I didn't ask him to."

"That's it, of course your PE and fine arts credits are being covered by dance …" Mr. Briggs turned around to face Taylor again, leaning forward and resting his elbows on his knees. "High school — it's great. It's educational, it's an opportunity to make friends, have new experiences, it can be a home away from home, but it's only all these things if you want it to be. So, Taylor, what are you doing here? What do you want to get out of sitting in class?"

"Um ..." Taylor shrugged.

"What do you think you are here for?"

"To graduate? Like, to get a high school diploma."

"Why?"

"Because I want to."

"Do you really want to? Look at these grades, Taylor. I want you to do something for me. I want you to go home, and think long and hard about why you're here. And if you think your time would be better spent doing something else, if you have something more productive that you could be doing instead of going to school, then maybe you should be doing that. Because, you sitting here learning nothing — it's not good for anybody, especially not you."

Taylor stared at Mr. Briggs, completely confused. "What do you mean?" she asked. "Like ... drop out?"

Mr. Briggs sighed. "Sometimes in life we are pushed into doing things at a certain time, in a certain way, just because everyone else is. It's not always the right thing to do. If you think that you could be spending your time better working at something else, Taylor, then I think you should do it. Dropping out of high school doesn't mean you aren't ever going to go *back* to school."

"Yeah." Taylor digested this slowly. The more she thought about it, the more it seemed to make sense. "And like — I could go back? If I wanted to?"

"Of course," Mr. Briggs said. "You could come back

here next year, or work online, or take adult education classes when you are older. There are so many options."

Taylor thought. Inside her, hope rose. *It would be so awesome. To not think about homework, and not worry about failing everything all the time. And then I could work harder at dance, and I would be really good …"*

"You should talk to your mother about it. Tell her to give me a call."

"Okay." Taylor got up to leave.

"If you have any ideas, or just want to talk, come and see me or give me a call, all right?"

"Okay. Thanks." Taylor left. She had a lot to think about.

Taylor walked around to the bus stop. Everyone else was already waiting there, and Michael and Chloe ran up to tell her how awesome her performance had been.

"Good job," Alexandra said, nodding at her. Taylor smiled. A "good job" from Alexandra meant it really had been good. She rose up on *demi pointe* and back down again, blushing.

Julian came running up late, and gave her a hug. "Good job, Tay," he said.

"Thanks!" said Taylor.

Taylor lay on the floor as she waited for class to start, listening to her iPod with her sweat towel spread over her face. She could feel the heat of her face, and exhaled, pushing the towel away from her mouth. "Are you dead?" Keiko asked above her.

"Yes, yes I am," Taylor answered. She could feel her back bones press into the studio floor, the grains of dirt sticking to her back. *If I didn't go to school, maybe I could take more classes in the morning with the Youth Company students.*

"Well, Mrs. Demidovski wants you in her office, so you'd better get undead."

Taylor jolted up. "Why? What? Why does she need me?"

Keiko shrugged. "I don't know. She just told me to get you."

Taylor got up and threw her sweat towel on the place on the floor that she wanted to stand to save her place, and walked quickly to the office. It wasn't just Mrs. Demidovski there, there was also Mr. Demidovski, and Julian. Gabriel ushered her in and closed the door behind her. She met Julian's eyes, but he shook his head slightly. He had no idea why they were there, either.

"Sit down," Gabriel instructed.

Taylor sat. Behind her, Gabriel tapped on his computer and pretended he wasn't there.

"You like Mr. Demidovski to coach you?" Mrs. Demidovski asked finally.

"Um, yeah, of course," Julian said quickly. Taylor nodded.

"You not maybe want someone else to coach you?" Mr. Demidovski asked.

"It is a great honour!" Mrs. Demidovski hissed at them. "Mr. Demidovski was one of the great dancers, and then he is the great teacher. He coached so many in the good companies now, so many they say: 'Thank you Mr. Demidovski, I cannot do without you.'"

Mr. Demidovski stared directly at Taylor. She could see her face reflected in his large brown eyes. "We give you so much at the academy," he said.

"Why you hate Mr. Demidovski?" Mrs. Demidovski snapped at her. "We give you every opportunity."

Taylor leaned back as the Demidovski's leaned forward, focusing on her. *Of course it's my fault*, she thought. *Couldn't possibly be the perfect Julian's fault.*

"I'm sorry," she said politely. "I don't understand. Me and Julian *do* want to be coached by you, Mr. Demidovski."

"Yeah," Julian chimed in. "We for sure do."

Mrs. Demidovski silently handed Julian a letter, and he and Taylor read it together.

Dear Mr. and Mrs. Demidovski,

I hope this letter finds you in good health. I have always greatly admired the fine training that Vancouver International Ballet Academy gives its students, and in the recent Spring Seminar that several of your students attended, two in particular caught my eye. I am writing to ask your permission to coach them on their variations for competition, since I of course do not want to interfere with any training they are currently receiving. The students I am inquiring about are Taylor Audley and Julian Reese, who have both also expressed an interest in studying with me. Please get back to me at your earliest convenience.

Sincerely, Theresa Bachman

Oh crap. Taylor looked up, her cheeks flushed slightly with guilt. "Well, you see, she like asked us, and then we said, 'maybe,' you know? We didn't mean we didn't want to study with you."

"Yeah," Julian nodded. "Don't worry, we really want to study with you —"

"Mrs. Demidovski does not worry!" Mrs. Demidovski snapped. "If you want to waste much money studying with teacher who does not know how to teach, is your business. We do not care."

Gabriel opened the door of the office, and Julian and Taylor exited, both making their way downstairs instinctively, away from the upstairs studios. They could hear the piano music start, and Mrs. Castillo begin to lead class in the right studio. Mr. Yu was shouting something at the younger students in the left studio. Taylor walked down the hallway with its many mirrors, and through to the stairs of the change room, Julian following her. She went into the girls' bathroom, and wiped her eyes which had already teared up, trying not to mess up her eyeliner. She felt someone watch her, and looked up. It was Julian. "This is the girl's bathroom," she informed him, hearing her voice break. "And you should get to class."

"Sorry," Julian said automatically. He came farther inside and sat on the sink counter. "So, what are we going to do?"

"I don't know," Taylor said honestly, also climbing up onto the counter. "What do you want to do?"

"Have privates with Theresa," Julian said without thinking.

"Well, the Demidovskis can't stop us from studying with one of the greatest ballet dancers in Canadian history."

"Yeah."

Taylor added more sparkles to her eyelids and fixed the clip in her hair. "I wonder how much she charges."

"Oh!" Julian said, slapping his forehead. "I never even thought about that!"

"Well, we can just ask her," Taylor pointed out. "So, you want to do this?"

"Yeah," said Julian. "I'm in."

"Let's go to class then." Taylor jumped off of the sink counter.

"So, you agree with me?" Julian clarified. "You want to have privates with her?"

"Yes," Taylor said, starting to smile. "Want to shake on it?"

"Yes," Julian said, grinning. They shook: slap Taylor on top, slap Julian on top, side, side, fist clasp, jazz hand. "We are sooo cool." They headed upstairs to class.

* * *

After class, Taylor walked out with Julian, Tristan, Kageki, and Keiko. "Let's go get bubble tea," Julian said suddenly. "We haven't done that since summer."

"That's because it's cold out," Tristan pointed out. But they started heading in the direction of Daun's anyway.

"Chinese buns ..." Taylor said, walking faster. "Good idea, Jules." They walked to Duan's and sat down in a booth, getting Kageki to order for them because it always came faster if he did it. The owners of Duan's didn't like the Caucasian students at the academy, always serving them last and trying to give them "good deals" that cost more than the original price.

"Smile," said Keiko, digging out her camera. Taylor grinned and flashed two peace signs at the camera, and then Keiko took a picture of everyone's food. Taylor started to giggle.

"What?" Keiko asked.

"This was a fun day," Taylor explained. "Oh, geez, do you realize it's almost time for auditions?"

Tristan nodded. "Me and Alexandra have planned which ones we are doing and everything," he explained. "We're carpooling." He looked at Julian. "You decided if you want to come with yet?"

Taylor thought quickly. "Or he can just come with us," she said quickly. "Cause we'll probably have more room."

"I'm not sure," Julian answered. "We can probably just wing it a little closer to the time, hey? I mean, it's not like it's tomorrow, they're mostly after YAGP, right? I don't even know if I'm doing any auditions."

"Let me know soon, though," Tristan prodded warningly. "Otherwise we might end up taking other people and not have a seat for you."

"Well, you could still just come with me," Taylor repeated.

"Guess what?" Keiko whispered to Taylor as the boys began to discuss something Mr. Yu had said during men's technique class. "Look."

Taylor looked over to where Keiko was looking. "Where?"

"Outside the window."

Taylor looked. Outside the window, Angela was walking, alone. Taylor giggled.

"What?" Tristan asked, suddenly paying attention.

Keiko pointed.

"Why does she even go to the academy?" Tristan said, disgusted. "She's *so* bad. Like, how did she even get accepted?"

"I heard the Demidovskis made her pay International fees," Kageki said, coming back with the bubble teas and buns. "Even though she's Canadian — because her parents are in Romania?"

Taylor sipped her strawberry bubble tea happily, chasing the tapioca balls with her hot pink straw. "I don't think Mr. Yu's corrected her, like, once," she said. She felt the cold chill her body, but the sugar made her happy. She lay her head on Keiko's shoulder, and they all sat quietly finishing their bubble teas and buns.

Chapter Eight

Alexandra Dunstan
No, I can't go see Marianas Trench perform today, I do ballet therefore I do not have a life ☹

Alexandra liked a lot of things that tended to disturb normal people: Catholicism (especially during the inquisition), William the Conqueror, MCR, the smell of sweat, and fixing her messed-up feet were a few. Particularly when they had huge water blisters. She sat on her quilt, a project she and her best friend at the time had made the summer before they had entered grade seven. She still loved the quilt, but hadn't talked to the friend in years. She couldn't remember how it was that she had ended up with the quilt. She stuck a disinfected needle through the skin of her toe and let the not-water seep out, dabbing it away with a Kleenex. *There, that's the last one.* She stuck her feet off the side of the bed into a large bowl of salt water to disinfect them and turned back to the book she was reading. In a quite matter-of-fact way it was called *The Pointe Book.* Which it was. Alexandra liked to read casually, she found it comforting reading about the different makes of *pointe* shoes and the short anecdotes from the dancers who wore them. Without this book, she might never have known that Pavlova's shoes were Capezio, or that the Royal Ballet liked their students to wear Freeds.

"Lexi, where are you?" Beth came through the door of Alexandra's bedroom, receiving the full benefit of her raised eyebrows. "Don't look at me like that. Where is your suitcase?"

"I'm not going."

Beth stared at her. "What do you *mean* you aren't going?"

Alexandra shrugged, staring at her mother and taking her feet out of the salt water. She felt a ripple of fear through her stomach and tried to ignore it. "I told you. I can't take that much time off."

"You are going to miss going to Mexico so you can make a point?"

"Mom, it's not about making a point. That's a whole week you're asking me to take off. A whole week of no classes, rehearsals — how am I supposed to catch up? Competition is almost here, I'd have to miss auditions, and I'd probably get kicked out of June show. I'm not going."

Alexandra had never seen Beth look so angry before. "Alexandra Noelle Dunstan, you are going to come with us, or we will pull you out of dance faster than you can breathe."

"Really? Would you really do that? How would you explain to everyone then, when I said I had to quit dance because you guys pulled me out after this many years of work?"

"I would tell the truth," Beth said, her face suddenly extremely ugly from the combination of anger and trying not to cry. "That you are a bulimic, out-of-control mess, and that you needed to get some perspective on life."

"That's not fair," Alexandra whispered, tears rolling down her cheeks. "I *want* to go. But I can't take that much time off!"

"Lexi, is this really what you want? To be the sort of person who would miss meeting her relatives for fear of missing a week of dance? This is the only time everyone can come!"

"Mom!" Alexandra looked at her, wishing she would just get it. "Don't you understand? I won't have a part in June show. I'll lose at competition. Everything will be screwed up!"

Beth thought for a moment. "Fine," she said finally. "You can stay by yourself. But when they come for my birthday in June, you had better be perfect the entire time they are here. Your family wants to meet you, and most of them haven't seen you since you were a cute little girl. I don't want their opinion of you to change." She left, and Alexandra lay face-first on her bed, her hands holding her stomach. She felt sick, but she knew the confrontation had been unavoidable. An entire week! And it probably would end up taking longer. *They will decide to go on a road trip, or someone will get sick or something stupid.* Lying on her side, she reached out and rescued her book, and started to read about how Paloma Herrera wore nothing on her feet to protect her from her *pointe* shoes. Alexandra bit her lip. She wore toe-pads, and spacers to separate her feet, and usually toe tape if she had a nasty blister (which was almost always). *All right, up. Time to go to school.* She sat up and put on her socks, set *The Pointe Book* down in order to pick up her backpack full of textbooks, and went downstairs. She wanted to eat the doughnut Justin had left on the kitchen counter, but it had too many calories and after her mother's comment she didn't feel like throwing it up. Instead, she grabbed a banana and ate it on the way to the bus stop, the cold air making it taste sweeter.

Alexandra ran up to school, unwrapping her coat and her scarf as she walked, hurrying. She was going to be late. She half ran up the stairs, ducked into the bathroom to smooth out her hair, and then slipped into her classroom. Grace had saved her a seat. Mr. Angelo stopped speaking for a moment. "Glad that you could join us, Ms. Dunstan."

"Sorry." Alexandra hung her coat on the back of her desk chair so that it would dry and pulled out her notebook, quickly writing down the date. Mr. Angelo was talking about Macbeth again. Alexandra thought he might need psychiatric help; every other grade eleven English class in the school had done Macbeth in one term, but it was second term and Mr. Angelo was still going. Alexandra didn't know how much more Shakespearean blood-bath analysis she could take. She began to write MACBETH in large, loopy cursive writing.

"Alexandra," Mr. Angelo called her. "Could you read Lady Macbeth for us?" Alexandra nodded and took the offered book from James Wong, who sat to her left. He pointed to the line where she was to start reading.

"'Consider it not so deeply.'"

She waited for the cool boy opposite her to finish reading Macbeth's part. He took longer than needed, acting it out to laughter from the class. Alexandra bit her lip, trying not to giggle. He was one of the theatre kids, and reading aloud was pretty much why he showed up to class.

"These deeds must not be thought/After these ways; so, it will make us mad," Alexandra enunciated clearly, in her best speaking voice. She looked at Mr. Angelo, and he nodded that yes, she could sit down. Alexandra sat, carefully not looking at everyone. She didn't like speaking in class at school; she never really knew what everyone thought of her, or if they thought of her at all. She began to draw a flower in her notebook growing out of the name Macbeth as Mr. Angelo continued to speak. She liked Shakespeare; she had a feeling that he didn't take himself too seriously. And he had a great sense of humour. She zoned in, listening as Anna spoke up to answer one of Mr. Angelo's many discussion questions.

"Well, I just think that was dumb," she was saying. "If Macbeth believed that, he must've been stupid. Did he grow up under a rock or something?" Alexandra put her head in her hands and rubbed her forehead. Eight-thirty in the morning and she already had a headache.

"Lexi, what do you think?" Mr. Angelo asked.

Alexandra looked up. "Um — I think that Macbeth was misled, but that it was ultimately his own fear at being nobody that made him crazy." The bell rang, and Alexandra got up, shoving her journal back in the bag as she got up for her next class.

"Hey, Lexi," Grace asked, leaving Anna and hurrying to catch up to Alexandra. "Do you think I could copy your homework for Bio?"

"Uh —" Alexandra thought. She didn't think they wouldn't be doing much in Bio today … "Sorry, Grace, I'm going to the Dance Centre to rehearse." She turned around and left Grace standing there, looking confused.

Alexandra fled down the winding staircase and out of McKinley, trying not to grin. Grace would get a zero on her assignment, and she knew that Mr. Ng would let her hand it in late if she told him that she had been rehearsing, because he never messed with Super Achiever students. He had once told them that he had hadn't wanted to be a biology teacher. In answer to what would he like to be instead, he had informed him that he'd like to be a hockey player "but then I can't stand up on skates and I'm skinny, so that wouldn't have worked," he had added mournfully.

Alexandra kept putting weight on her left foot and then taking it off again as she rode on the Canada Line. Her ankle was hurting again, sudden jabbing pain without warning, and she couldn't tell whether it was going to be okay on *pointe* today or not. It kept getting better and then worse again, and she couldn't seem fix it. She'd been putting Tiger Balm on, but it didn't seem to do anything. She'd gone to the physiotherapist with her mom; the physiotherapist said that Alexandra needed to strengthen her feet and calves and advised her to use a Thera-Band every day. A few weeks after that, Alexandra had gone to St. Paul's Hospital by herself to get it X-rayed. It showed that a tendon had been seriously overstretched, and the doctor advised her to take at least six weeks off.

Alexandra had rolled her eyes at that advice: it was what doctors always said. "Take some time off, rest it." If they really didn't know how to fix it, they asked you to consider quitting dance in favour of swimming. No, there was no way that Alexandra was going to take some time off right before competition and *Coppelia* casting. There was no realistic hope that the Demidovskis would understand if she took few weeks off, either. They would think she was just being lazy, stupid, or both, and it would definitely affect her future casting. She hadn't told her mom about the visit to St Paul's; Beth would have insisted that Alexandra follow the doctor's advice. She had been on a good-mother kick recently, and Alexandra really didn't feel like yet another argument. She got off the bus, signed in, and paid at the front desk of the Dance Centre, then took the elevator up and thankfully stepped in to the huge, empty studio. Suddenly she could breathe properly again. She dropped her bag at the side and did a spontaneous and messy *jeté* across the floor, landing horribly and not caring. She laughed as she straightened up; her ankle was feeling better today. The clock ticked, and Alexandra got to work. She had an hour before she had to get to her first class of the day at the academy.

Alexandra hurried out of the building, the sweat on her body turning cold the moment she went outside, making her shiver inside her coat. If only she could get her *pirouettes* cleaner — it seemed to be that she could never land the last one if she made it a quadruple, and a triple was just too lame for a finishing *pirouette*. She frowned as she thought of Kaitlyn; she'd done nine and landed them effortlessly the other day. And Kaitlyn was two years younger than her … the bus came and Alexandra got on it, making her way absently to a clear seat and taking her phone out of her pocket.

As she passed the meth head sitting in the bench in front she noticed her body. *Nice*, she thought admiringly. *Nothing like meth to make you skinny. Too bad it kills you, too.* She watched the girl out of the corner of her eye, admiring the line of her slim shoulder blades. Suddenly the girl turned around, and Alexandra quickly dropped her eyes to the floor.

"I like your eyes," said the girl, leaning forward to see Alexandra better and nearly toppling out of her seat in the process.

Alexandra gave her a small and what she hoped was a discouraging smile and started playing with her phone.

The girl turned around in her seat to face Alexandra, gazing fascinated at her eyes with their sparkly eyeshadow and eyeliner. "Sparkly …" she said, clutching the back of her seat in excitement. Her thin, white, hands were like small claws, and Alexandra shivered.

"Hmmm," Alexandra replied. She reached in her bag for her Tylenol since her legs were aching, and then thought better of taking it out. *Pills are pills.* She sighed and wondered if the meth head was going to stay on the bus long, She didn't show any signs of moving.

The girl lost interest in Alexandra for a minute, and took off her left shoe. She looked at it warily and then suddenly decided that it was dangerous and kicked it under her seat. She turned back to Alexandra. "What's your name?"

"Ale … Lexi," Alexandra said quickly.

"So pretty … like sparkles. You're *pretty*," said the girl, tilting her head from side to side. She began to rock from side to side every time she tilted her head, first slowly and then faster. At that moment the bus driver called out the stop name. To Alexandra's surprise, he got up out of his seat and walked up to the meth head.

"Hey, you," he said loudly, trying to snap her out of her rocking trance. The girl ignored him. "You said this was your stop. You said you were getting off at Hastings," he continued, a little louder. The whole bus turned around to watch, and Alexandra blushed, wishing she could move. The girl was still facing her so everyone was also staring at Alexandra. "You've been on this bus for a whole loop now, time to get off," said the bus driver, more for the other passengers' benefit than the girl's since she was obviously not listening to him. "Come on," he said, grabbing her by the arm. "Off you go." At this the girl woke up and started screaming expletives at him. "Yes, right," said the bus driver, unmoved. "Do you want me to call the police? Didn't think so. Now off you get." The girl got off, still screaming and now starting to cry.

Alexandra stared after her in fascinated horror. "Wait," she choked out, "she forgot her shoe ..." But it was too late, the bus driver was pulling out and the girl was running down the street with one shoe on, the shoelaces flapping as she went.

"Next stop is Granville and Georgia," the bus driver called out. "Granville, next stop."

Alexandra got out her bottle of Tylenol and took two extra-strength tablets, swallowing them without water. The passengers around her stared at her suspiciously, and Alexandra slumped down into her seat, embarrassed. She plugged in her iPod, not wanting to feel them staring at her, listening to Noah and the Whale play "5 Years Time."

"There'll be sun, sun, sun," she sang under her breath, staring out the window. The bus stopped, and Alexandra timed getting out of her seat exactly with the lurch of the bus so she used the momentum to swing out the door. "Thanks," she called behind her, beginning to walk to the academy.

As Alexandra stretched in the studio she sensed a body hovering over her. She rolled over onto her back, annoyed, and looked up. "What?" she snapped. She saw it was Julian. "What do you want, Jules?"she asked in a nicer voice.

"Oh, hey," Julian said, sitting down beside her. "Um, I was wondering if maybe next time you dropped in on Leah's class I could come, too? I really want to work on my contemporary, you know? My ballet's getting a lot better, but ..."

Grace came over and sat by them. "You know if you have ballet, contemporary's pretty easy," she said. "At least the contemporary you would do in a ballet company."

Alexandra nodded while disagreeing. "Not really," she said. "I mean, yeah, you need ballet for technique, but there is lots you can only get from contemporary."

Grace laughed, high up in her throat. "Well, you love contemporary, Lexi, so that's why you think so."

Julian looked at her. "I like contemporary, too," he said. "It's awesome. I don't just want to be doing the classics my whole life. I want to be able to do new stuff, too."

"Do you know what I hate?" Grace asked leisurely, sliding into the splits and pulling her back foot up toward her head. "People who train super-hard for contemporary, like they are going to have a career dancing jazz or something. Okay, yeah, if you want to dance on a cruise ship for the rest of your life or something, but really —"

Julian sat up, frowning. "What, are you saying that training for contemporary is a waste of time?"

"No," Grace said. "I'm saying that training solely for contemporary is a waste of time. It's just not practical."

Julian and Alexandra looked at each other, bonded in disbelief. "So," Alexandra said, "a ballet dancer and a jazz dancer walk into a bar, and the ballet dancer says: 'you need to pick a more stable career path?'" Julian giggled appreciatively, and Grace looked annoyed.

Mrs. Castillo walked in, and they got up, heading for the *barre.* "I like your towel," Alexandra said to Julian as they set their towels and water bottles down at the ends of the barre.

"Thanks," said Julian, embarrassed. "My dad's girlfriend Daisy made it. Not the actual towel bit, but the dye."

Alexandra picked it up and looked at it carefully. It had a tie-dyed blue background with a bright sun in the centre of two trees. "She's really good," she commented.

"Yeah, I think so, too." Julian nodded. "But you might want to put that down, I haven't washed it since last class."

"Ew." Alexandra quickly dropped it as Mrs. Castillo came over and began showing them the first exercise.

"Alexandra!" Mrs. Castillo snapped as Alexandra stretched out her ankle, trying to find a way to roll through without making it hurt. "Must be attention me. Why nobody ever attention to me? No respect. Mr. Moretti, you respect. Mr. And Mrs. Demidovski, you respect. Mrs. Castillo, no respect."

"We respect you, Mrs. Castillo," Tristan called out.

Mrs. Castillo's face lit up and she smiled, breaking into a choky smoker's laugh. "Good boy, good boy," she said. She walked over to him and slapped his stomach. "Good lunch?" She looked in the mirror at herself. "Mrs. Castillo is too skinny," she said mournfully, beginning to laugh again. "I too old, makes me too skinny." Her students giggled. "Maybe next time I go to the bathroom, fall in the toilet because too skinny," Mrs. Castillo continued, encouraged by their laughter. "Whoosh! No more Mrs. Castillo." They giggled still, but a little nervously.

"Don't fall in the toilet, Mrs. Castillo," Tristan said charmingly. "We would miss you."

"Oh, you miss me yelling at you?" Mrs. Castillo asked, her eyebrows raised. "Good. Must be yell if want to be good dancer. Okay, begin." She clapped her hands together, making a surprisingly loud noise, and George began playing. They began the *plies*, doing a very improvised version as no one had really gotten the exercise except Aiko, who always paid attention.

Alexandra waited for fifteen minutes after class before calling her mother. "Mom? Is someone coming to pick me up? Because Grace already left, so I can't get a ride with her now."

Beth groaned. "Oh, sweetie — I thought your dad was going to pick you up, but I forgot he has a work meeting. Can you take the bus? I'm waiting for Emma to finish practice now." Alexandra could hear the echoing shouts of Emma's gymnastics studio in the background, and sighed.

"Okay," she agreed. "Lame. K, bye." She hung up the phone and went outside to wait for the bus. Julian was already waiting there, with his homestay brother Leon.

"Hey guys," she said. She set her heavy bag down on the bench and massaged her sore arm, yawning. Leon nodded. He was too cool to talk; he was in the Youth Company. Alexandra didn't have much respect for him, he still homestayed with Mr. Yu and was twenty-two years old. He hadn't even started to audition for anything yet — he had auditioned for Vancouver Ballet and not made it past the second cut. Alexandra had very high standards for other people and she didn't like it when they didn't live up to them. Which was why she occasionally listened to "Watching the Wheels Go By," and comforted herself with the fact that John Lennon had obviously not listened to his own advice; after all, he had been a Beatle, and John Lennon. That sort of thing didn't happen to people who sat and watched wheels go by.

"'Sup?" Julian nodded. He was sitting on the back of the bus stop bench, carefully balancing with his feet on the seat.

Alexandra shrugged. She went over and sat on the bench next to him. "Ready for competition?" she asked to fill the silence.

"No," Julian said. He rubbed his head. "Well, I don't think I'll ever feel ready. I'm excited for mine and Taylor's contemporary *pas de deux*, though."

"Yeah?" Alexandra covered up another yawn. "Who'd you get to choreograph it for you?"

Julian looked nervous. "Uh, I did."

Alexandra looked at him, surprised. "Nice," she said. "That's pretty brave, doing your own work." Leon blew some cigarette smoke toward them and she glared at him, annoyed.

"Yeah, that's why I didn't tell people," Julian admitted. "It's way scarier than doing someone else's work."

"What did the Demidovskis say?"

"I didn't tell them." They both laughed.

"Awkward," Alexandra said. "Can you picture that conversation? Who choreograph? You? No, no good, must be teacher!" Her voice pitched to mimic the voices of the academy owners.

"Exactly. That's why I didn't tell them."

"How's working with Taylor?" Alexandra asked. "I can't imagine having to have privates with her, to be honest. No offence."

Julian shrugged. "It's fine. She's pretty good. I mean, not as good as you, obviously, but who *is* as good as Alexandra Dunstan?" he said, half-joking.

Alexandra smiled. "No-one, ob-vi-ously," she answered, playing along. A street lamp across from them suddenly switched on, and Alexandra blinked in surprise. "Where is the fricking bus?"

"I think I'm just going to walk to the station," Julian decided.

"Me, too." They started to walk, leaving Leon behind them, leaning moodily on the bus stop pole blowing smoke into the air.

"So, what are you doing this summer?" Julian asked, breaking the awkward silence.

"I haven't decided," Alexandra said, shoving her hands in her pockets. "I need to get out of here, and into a different school, a different city."

"What do your parents want you to do?"

Alexandra looked him, frowning. "What do you mean? It's my choice."

"Yeah, but they're going to be paying for it, aren't they?"

"So? If I didn't study ballet, they'd still have to pay for, like, university or something, right?" Julian shrugged. Alexandra wondered what he was thinking. He suddenly looked very disapproving, and she didn't like it.

"So, how are you and Taylor's privates coming along?" Alexandra asked. "I noticed that you don't have many scheduled."

"Uh," said Julian. Alexandra waited impatiently, as he looked uncomfortable. "Um, we're also being coached by someone else."

Alexandra snapped her head around to look at him. "What? Who?"

"Theresa Bachman."

"What?"

"Yeah. It's pretty sweet, actually," Julian started to babble. "She's really cool and nice, and a lot different from Mr. Yu and Mr. Moretti and stuff."

Alexandra digested this. "But, she's not — I mean, she was a good dancer and stuff, but she's not exactly a *teacher*, is she?"

"What do you mean?" Julian looked confused. "She's good at teaching."

"Well, if you like her ..." Alexandra trailed off.

"I do," Julian said, jutting his chin forward firmly. Alexandra rolled her eyes behind his back. Julian was so obvious when he decided he liked a teacher, or a dance, or a student — he would become fiercely obstinate about that person or thing, and argue why he was right until everyone else was completely sick of the subject. Alexandra had had the misfortune to sit next to Julian and Tristan the day Tristan had tried to argue that there was nothing better about organic produce. Alexandra had wanted to punch them both in the face by the time they had gotten to the academy.

"Well, I have nothing against her," Alexandra reassured Julian quickly, and he relaxed. They reached the station, and separated, Alexandra catching the train north to Waterfront station and Julian taking the train south up to 49th Avenue. *I wonder if Julian is actually any good at choreographing?* Alexandra thought as she got on the train. *You just never know with him. But he can't be better than Leah ...*

Chapter Nine

Julian Reese
Time for my first competition ever? Yes, yes I think so :D

Julian picked up his toothbrush and frowned; the bristles were damp. Someone in his homestay kept using his toothbrush, and he was betting that it was Leon. He finished washing his face and walked into the kitchen. It was full — apparently everyone was late getting started this morning, not just him. Mao and Keiko were sitting at the table eating cereal, Mr. Yu was drinking black coffee standing up, still in his bathrobe, Leon was lying with his head in his arms on the table, and Mrs. Yu was cutting up something that was probably edible that Julian didn't recognize on her huge wooden cutting board.

Mrs. Yu started to sing a song in Mandarin, and Julian winced. He didn't mind Mrs. Yu's singing, it was pretty good, just not at seven in the morning. He poured himself a bowl of cereal, resigned to the fact that it was Cheerios after almost ten months of living with the Yus, and started to eat. Around him, everyone was also already up and eating, including Mr. Yu. Mr. Yu suddenly looked up, and Julian stopped eating, looking at him.

Mr. Yu grunted. "You taking the bus to theatre?"

Julian looked at him, surprised. "Um, no, Leon is driving me. His ankle is bad, he can't go to class today."

"Okay, good," Mr. Yu nodded to him. "Good luck. Make us look good, hey?"

"I'll try."

Julian followed Leon out the door, trying not to slip on the wet steps. It was still fairly dark outside. Leon slid into the front, starting the car to try and warm it up. Julian shoved his suitcase in the back seat and got in the front beside him, shivering as the first blast of the heat hit his body. "You have to get a warmer jacket, man," Leon said disapprovingly.

Julian shook his head, teeth chattering. "I like this one," he insisted. He was wearing a thick blue hoodie underneath an old fake leather jacket of his dad's.

Leon changed the CD, and an old Bright Eyes song began playing.

"What are you doing this summer, Leon?" Julian said suddenly.

Leon shrugged. "Staying here, probably. Getting ready to audition."

Julian nodded. He knew Leon had already tried to audition before, but hadn't gotten in anywhere, and that Leon was probably not going to get a job since he was already twenty-two. He liked Leon: he just didn't understand why Leon didn't realize this simple fact. Julian had promised himself that if he didn't have a job by at least eighteen or nineteen he was going to move on, do something else. Probably still in dance, like a choreographer or a teacher, but he never wanted to be old and still auditioning.

"What about you?"

"I don't know. Tristan and Taylor think I should audition for summer intensives in the States with them. But Mr. Yu said I should just stay at the academy and train."

Leon shook his head and laughed.

"What?" Julian asked, starting to smile. He shifted his feet closer to the heat vent. His runners were always wet these days, he got home so late and left so early in the morning that they had no time to dry out.

"I just think it's funny, that's all," Leon said. "The way you actually care what other people think you should do."

"Why wouldn't I?" Julian asked.

Leon didn't answer, concentrating on turning on to the highway. Looking out the window, everything appeared blurry to Julian, the fog covering the grey highway and the rising sun partially obscured by the rain clouds.

Julian sat back in his seat, sulking. He felt patronized, and he didn't like it.

"I'm just teasing you," Leon said. "Relax."

"It's fine." Julian shrugged.

"You excited?" Leon asked.

"Yeah. But I'm so nervous," Julian admitted. "I know it's just a local competition, but I feel like if I don't win here I definitely won't win at YAGP."

"Don't worry," Leon said easily. "Today's your first competition, nobody expects you to do well."

Julian didn't answer, restlessly tapping his foot. He suddenly wished he had practised more, or not choreographed his own solo, or found a cooler costume, or that he could stop feeling so nervous. "I don't even really want to do competitions," he said suddenly. "I want to be more anti-competitions, you know? Like, I want to travel everywhere and dance in different places, choreograph — that's what I want."

"Why are you doing so many competitions this year, then?"

Julian paused, thinking. "I … I just want to know how good I am, I guess," he said. "And I don't really know what I want. If a ballet company offered me a position, I probably would say yes, you know? It's just, I don't know if I would really fit in with a ballet company."

Leon nodded, looking a little ill. Talking about auditioning was clearly an insensitive topic of conversation. Julian kept talking, though; he needed to talk to someone. "If I did get into a ballet company, and everything was good, what? Do I just stay there? I'm not like Alexandra or Tristan, I don't know if I could do that, slowly working my way up. But it would be nice to have a company taking care of everything for me."

Leon turned up the volume on his stereo.

"Can I switch this?" Julian asked. "No offence, but it's kind of depressing."

Leon shrugged, and Julian turned on the radio to The Peak. They began listening to "The Stand," by Mother Mother, but before the song could finish Leon had pulled in front of the large suburban community centre where the competition was being held. "Good luck."

"Thanks for driving me." Julian grabbed his bag and scrambled out of the car.

"Don't forget your CD!" Leon called after him.

"Oh crap, sorry!" Julian turned back and grabbed it, slipping it into his hoodie pocket. He slammed the old car door shut and started walking toward the theatre as Leon drove away.

It was still cold outside, and the morning sun was just barely up, the dew making the pavement sparkle and the car oil in the puddles form pretty rainbows. Julian could feel excitement spread through him with every step. He hadn't actually been on stage since *The Nutcracker*, and being on stage was Julian's favourite part of dancing. Besides, at *The Nutcracker* he'd been feeling sick so that hadn't really been fun. He had a feeling that today was going to be awesome. There was a sign on the glass lobby doors that said VANCOUVER FESTIVAL OF DANCE. Julian pushed the door open and stepped inside.

Inside the huge lobby was almost empty, except for a woman reading a book behind the counter of a concession stand. Julian walked up to her and stood in front of the counter, waiting.

She ignored him.

"Hey," he said quietly.

She flipped a page.

"Excuse me?" he asked politely but louder. "I'm competing today, do you know —"

"Down that way, turn left," the woman said pointing farther down the lobby without lookin' up. Julian nodded and walked quickly off in the direction she had indicated. There was a set of stairs, and he looked back at the woman, unsure if he was supposed to go down them. She was still absorbed in her book, and he shrugged, beginning to walk down the stairs. He checked his cellphone; he was early and still had time to get lost.

"JULIAN!" Julian almost fell over as Taylor jumped onto him, hugging him. "Come on, we're all set up in here!"

"Isn't this the girls' change room?" Julian asked, stepping inside. Keiko was busy turning on every one of the bright lights that surrounded all the change-room mirrors. Excellent for illuminating a face to put makeup on it, these lights had remarkable heating qualities, and Julian could feel the room start to warm up already. Julian set down his bag beside Taylor and dropped to the floor, cracking both of his hips.

"I like your jeans, are they new?" Alexandra asked, looking at his reflection in her mirror as she applied foundation.

"Sort of. Leon gave them to me," Julian explained. A mother walked out of the change room with her young daughter and gave Julian a disapproving look. Julian stuck his tongue out at her back as she walked out the door.

"That woman is fat," Keiko said watching the mother leave.

"*Aishteru*, Keiko," Taylor said, giggling.

"What does that mean?" Julian asked.

"I love you," Taylor explained.

"*Aishteru* you too, Taylor," said Keiko. She began to work with her Thera-Band, stretching out her feet. "Ah, it is so cold today!"

Julian shrugged. "I feel hot," he said.

"You're always hot," Taylor said shrugging.

"Ha ha, you called me hot," Julian laughed.

"Soooo immature!"

A girl stepped in and looked around, seeing only academy students. "Oh," she said. She stepped out again, and they all laughed.

"I love how we, like, take up an entire change room," Anna said.

"Uh, yeah," said Julian. He pulled off his jeans and slipped into his sweatpants, beginning to stretch. "Are you sure I'm allowed in here?"

"No."

"All right then. If someone yells at me, it's your fault."

Tristan ducked in the door. "Anna, your mother wants you. Julian, why are you here so late?"

"I'm here an hour early."

"No comment. Karen wants to see you, now."

"Who's Karen?"

"One of the people who runs this festival. She has to check off that you're here and stuff."

"Okay, coming, can you, like, show me who she is?" Julian stood up and followed Tristan out of the change room, his feet cold on the cement floor. He followed Tristan down a hallway, past other change rooms with dancers of all ages warming up, through a small room with dancers that he recognized from Spring Seminar warming up.

"Hey," he said in passing.

There was a chorus of "nice to see you again," and "hey Jules," and then they were going up a narrow set of stairs to the stage.

It was dark and quiet backstage, very different from the jumbled confusion and noise that Julian was used to from the academy's performances. There was an old woman with short grey hair wearing a mint-green pantsuit who was writing in the corner. Tristan ignored her and walked onto the stage where the lights were already shining brightly. There a woman dressed all in black sat drinking tea. She had large pearl earrings, short dyed-brown hair, and pink lipstick.

"Here he is, Karen," Tristan said. He jumped off the stage and landed in front of the audience seats. "This is Julian Reese."

"Oh, hello," said Karen, looking up. "You're late."

"Sorry," said Julian. "I thought that my solo was at ten."

"It is," Karen said disapprovingly. "I'll just check you off on my list here — there we are." She found his name on the paper in front of her and carefully made a mark on it with her pencil. "Don't disappear now, we need you backstage in half an hour."

Julian nodded. "Okay. I'll just — go get changed." He walked quickly back to the change rooms. "Do I have to wear makeup?" he asked suddenly, pausing as he did up his vest.

"Yes." Taylor answered as she carefully painted on liquid eyeliner.

"But the stage is so small, and the audience is seated really close to me."

"You *have* to wear makeup, Julian," Taylor and Tristan said together.

Julian grabbed the makeup sponge and started trying to put some foundation on. It looked streaky over his naturally flushed cheeks.

"Here," Tristan said sighing. He expertly flipped over Taylor's makeup bottle and put a bit on the sponge, grabbing Julian's shoulder to stop his head from moving as he rubbed it on his face. "You have to cover up your blush to put blush on. Your natural blush looks fake."

"Uh, what?"

As he waited in the wings, Julian could feel his heart rate speed up. He wished he had time to go outside for a moment and get some air, but there wasn't enough time to duck out. He could feel his hands shaking slightly with nerves. He walked over to the pile of rosin on the floor backstage and ground a bit under his feet into his canvas shoes, and then prepared, beginning to *pirouette. One, two, three* — and then he landed. Good; he hadn't put too much rosin on, he could still turn easily. He adjusted his vest. It felt unnatural on his chest. It was so hot backstage. He could feel sweat already trickling down his back and chest and he hadn't even danced yet. In the corner, Tristan was listening to his variation on his iPod and marking it. Finally it was time to begin. There were only Julian, Tristan, Kageki, and two other boys from different schools competing that day. Kageki looked calm, repeatedly going over small sections of his solo. The lights dimmed in the audience, and Kageki walked over, first on the list of competitors.

"Kageki Sato?" the lady in the pantsuit whispered. "Start off?"

Kageki nodded and stepped close to the curtain, waiting for his music to start. He began with an astoundingly high jump, and Julian stared at him in surprise, moving closer to the wings as he watched. He hadn't noticed how much Kageki had been improving this year until now. He knew that Kageki worked hard, but it had never really occurred to him that Kageki was really good. Julian realized that he was. His jumps were higher than Tristan's, and although he was not flexible, he had gotten much stronger in the last couple of months. Julian watched in amazement as he pirouetted once, twice, three, four, five … and then landed perfectly. Kageki finished his solo with a grin, and bowed to loud applause from the sparse audience.

"Julian?" the pantsuit lady whispered, startling him as she suddenly appeared at his elbow. "You're second up."

Julian nodded, waiting in the wings and trying to breathe as he waited for the adjudicator to stop writing notes about Kageki. He heard the tinkle of the small bell the adjudicators were given on their desk to signal that the next solo could begin, and Julian walked on stage. He waited for his music.

He began late, not hearing the first beat until too late as the CD player was playing his music more quietly than Kageki's music. He loved this variation so much — Theresa had let Taylor and Julian pick their own solos and *pas de deux*, thinking that they would do better if they picked what they liked. Julian had picked a variation from *La Bayadere*, which let him use the same costume as the one he wore for their *pas de deux*. They were doing *Le Corsaire* for their *pas de deux*.

This variation made Julian feel like he was flying, and he could feel the huge grin on his face. He still couldn't do much of the variation very cleanly, but he danced the harder parts very enthusiastically. He finished three pirouettes with a wobble, but was still smiling as he ran off stage. He heard clapping. *Oh crap* … He ran back on stage, bowed, and ran off again.

"You forgot to bow, didn't you?" Tristan asked him, looking disbelieving.

"Never," said Julian laughing. He watched one of the boys he didn't know wait nervously in the wings. He could feel buoyant glee filling him up. That was fun. He loved being on stage, it was the most awesome thing ever. The adrenalin rush was incomparable.

He went up to the pantsuit lady. "Am I allowed to sit in the audience?" he whispered.

"Yes, dear," she whispered back. "But be quiet."

Julian nodded and hurried out of the backstage. He couldn't just go through the stage now that the competition had started. He snuck up behind Taylor and Jessica. "Hey," he whispered, sliding into the seat beside Taylor.

"Hey," Taylor said, smiling at him.

Julian stared at her, confused. *That's it? "Hey?" How did I do?*

The bell tinkled and it was Tristan's turn. Julian sat back to watch silently, Taylor resting her head on his shoulder. Julian held his breath without realizing it as he watched Tristan begin his solo, the prince's variation from *Sleeping Beauty*. Tristan wasn't as strong as Kageki, but his muscles were less bulky, more fluid, and his body was more flexible. His extensions were extremely high for a boy, and his jumps were clean. They weren't as high or exciting as Kageki's, or as happy as Julian's, but they had a fluid cat-like quality that reminded Julian of Vladimir Malakhov.

Tristan bowed and ran off, and Julian felt himself deflate. There was something obviously different between his performance and Tristan's. Tristan's had a professional quality to it, a cleanness, a sense that he could exactly repeat any moment of his variation upon being asked, whereas how Julian performed his variation was largely up to luck or how he felt at the second he was dancing that beat. Julian realized that Tristan had thought about and rehearsed every second, every shift in emotion or performance, each transfer of weight or landing. The something different between their two solos was the difference in hours and hours of work between them. In fact, Julian had only practised his solo full out maybe five times on his own time (not in a private with a teacher) and that had only been because Taylor had guilted him into it while they had been rehearsing their *pas de deux* together.

Julian clapped so hard that his hands hurt. "He was good, right?" a grandmother sitting next to them asked. "I liked him."

"Yeah," Taylor and Julian said together. "He was really good."

"I thought you smiled more though, dear," she told Julian. She settled back down in her seat, going back to her crossword puzzle as the adjudicator shuffled his notes and stood up.

"Good job, me. I smiled," Julian muttered to himself.

"I have to go backstage," Taylor told him, shaking him off her shoulder.

"All right, fine." He shifted over a seat and leaned on Jessica instead. "Your shoulder hurts, it's too boney." She giggled.

Julian nodded. He noticed the adjudicator get up with his papers, and remembered he had to be backstage to get his placing. "Oh, crap!" he quickly jumped up and ran down the theatre, steps, disappearing backstage.

They filed onstage, waiting in a line for the adjudicator to come down. Julian stood in first position. He blinked — the lights were really bright. He began to sway, left … right …

"Stop it," Tristan hissed, poking him in the stomach with his finger. They were standing close enough together that he could do it without being too obvious. On the other side of Julian, Kageki just giggled. There was a commotion up at the main doors to the audience, and they all looked up. Julian saw Mr. Yu's silhouette. He walked in, so tall that that his head almost touched the top of the door. He put his hand to his forehead, peering out to the stage. Recognizing his students, he waved at them, and went to sit down, stepping over top of the rows of seats instead of walking in between them. He found a seat he liked and sat in it, putting his legs up on the back of the row of seats in front of him.

"He is so lucky Mr. Demidovski isn't here to see him," Tristan whispered, low enough that only Julian could hear him. Julian nodded, grinning as he saw their adjudicator glare at Mr. Yu as he walked past him.

The adjudicator was not very old, but he had an air of determined maturity. He opened his mouth and Julian hoped that he just told them who got what right away.

"My name is Josep Glass." He looked around at the almost empty theatre. "I won't bore you with my resume, I'll save that for the afternoon audience," he said dryly. "Suffice it to say that I am fully qualified and competent enough to critique you. Good job, dancers, there were some nice moments in all of your solos this morning." He looked down and began to read from his sheet of paper, squinting at the handwriting. "Julian Reese, third place."

Julian felt his face fall. He walked over and got his paper, forcing a smile that dropped as soon as he got back to his place in line. He stood there listening to him continue.

"Kageki Sato, second place." Kageki took his paper with a huge grin on his face, and returned to the line, bobbing up and down on the balls of his feet.

"Tristan Patel. First place." Tristan smiled confidently as he walked up and took the piece of paper, meeting Josep's eyes as he took it and nodding his head in thanks.

Josep handed out placings in other categories, and then they all filed off stage. "Is that it?" Julian asked.

"No, you can pick up a critique comment sheet from the box outside, too," Tristan explained. "Out in the lobby."

"Right," Julian said. "Congratulations." He went down to the change room and began to get changed into his street clothes, intending to go back into the theatre and watch Taylor's performance. He shoved the bag of makeup that Tristan and Taylor had helped him buy in his backpack, along with his sweaty tights, and folded up his costume neatly to ease the guilt at having not brought a costume bag to protect it. He knew Cromwell Gilly would have killed him if he'd seen what Julian was doing to his costume.

The lobby was mostly empty. Everyone had already gone into the theatre to watch the girls' competition. He paused, deliberating. Now that he was done, he just really wanted to get out of there and go home. He walked over to a lady who looked like she was helping out with the competition. "Hey," he said. "I was supposed to pick up a critique or something?"

"Name?"

"Julian Reese."

"Here you go, dear. Congratulations." Julian took the paper from her and walked away, opening it up and reading as he walked. It was a series of comments on his solo in bullet form.

* Keep your sternum forward.
* Not enough plie in your preparation for tour jeté or pirouettes, don't anticipate.
* Turn out your arabesque.
* Nice floating quality in your jumps.
* Nice lift to your jumps, but be careful of your form. Use the whole stage.
* You kept a lovely sense of stage presence and expression throughout the solo. This added a lot to your performance.

He stared at it, trying to wrest more than there was from the page. He wasn't sure what he had been looking for, but it wasn't this. He had, for reasons unknown to himself, cherished a hope that Josep would have written something more along the lines of:

> *Julian, you are that rare find, a truly naturally gifted and brilliant dancer. At such a young age you have managed accomplish more as an artist than the top dancers at twice your age. Please see enclosed your offer for a soloist position at American Ballet Theatre or the Royal Ballet, the choice is yours.*

Well, perhaps not exactly like that, but closer to that. Julian felt a bit disappointed. *Well, he said I have a nice stage presence*, he thought to himself, shrugging off his sadness with reality. He walked out of the theatre, past the parking lot toward a cement structure surrounded by tall grass and some scraggy trees. He had honestly believed that he would get first, he told himself as he sat there. The sun was shining finally, and the spot of cement he was sitting on was almost dry. *I'll do better at YAGP*, he decided. *If I just work harder ...* He took out a joint he had saved in his makeup bag and lit it, sitting on the grass. He just needed some time to himself, space to think. He had been so busy lately he hadn't realized how fast everything was going by. In a couple more weeks he was going to be in California. In a few months he was going to be finished grade eleven. He needed to work as hard as he could now, at dance, at school — he let the smoke rest in his lungs, and stared out at the sun as it sparkled on the grass. In the bottom of his stomach was the gloom that came from the truth: he could have done better. He knew it, even if nobody else knew it; and that was the part of his loss that hurt. He knew in his heart that he could be better than Tristan, but he hadn't put the time in. He hung his head between his legs, trying to block out the thoughts that were flooding his brain, his self-accusatory missives of hate. It was over. There was nothing he could do about what was past; he just had to do better next time.

Chapter Ten

Kaitlyn Wardle
Happy B-day Julian Reese! Ur old now ;)

Kaitlyn hopped from one foot to another as she waited for the bus. Her hands were freezing, even though she was wearing gloves and had her hands shoved in the pockets of her coat, and her feet were numb.

Taylor was telling an extremely unimpressed Jessica about her jeans. "People keep telling me that these jeans look really good on me, but I, like, don't know what they mean!"

"Maybe they mean those jeans look good on you?" Jessica said dryly, raising her eyebrows.

"Well, yeah, but, like, I'm a person, and these are jeans? Why are they hot on *me?* And I, like, don't have an ass!"

Kaitlyn pulled out her iPod, opting to be antisocial over listening to Taylor for one more moment. She turned the volume on low; she knew everyone would tease her so badly if they knew what she was listening to: she had downloaded an entire playlist of Selena Gomez and Miley Cyrus music.

"Kaitlyn."

Kaitlyn was busy humming along to "Liberty Walk."

"Kaitlyn!"

"What?" Kaitlyn quickly took out her earphones.

"Did you remember Julian's present?"

Kaitlyn nodded. "Of course."

"What did you get him?"

Kaitlyn frowned. She didn't think it was really any of Taylor's business what she had got Julian. "Starbucks gift card."

"For how much?"

"Taylor, seriously, why do you care? It's not your present."

"I just want to make sure everything is perfect." Taylor shrugged. "And I think he'll like a Starbucks gift card — even though it wasn't on the list that I gave you."

Kaitlyn didn't even try to not roll her eyes. Taylor had handed out an extremely detailed list of presents that Julian would probably like, written out in bullet point with purple gel pen. *Maybe she wouldn't be failing if she put as much effort into school as she did on that list,* Kaitlyn thought. Thinking about Taylor's grades made her feel better about her own; she'd gotten a C on her in-class essay on *The Curious Incident of the Dog in the Night-time.*

"Now, remember, meet me outside after class and pretend that you don't know anything about his birthday before that," Taylor ordered.

Jessica wandered off to meet Grace and Anna — she hadn't been invited to this birthday party. In fact, Kaitlyn didn't know who all had been invited. "Who's coming?" she asked.

"Me, you, Keiko, Tristan, and Julian, obviously," Taylor answered.

"Not Kageki?" Kaitlyn raised her eyebrows. "He's, like, one of Julian's best friends."

Taylor shrugged. "My mom said I was only allowed to invite four people over," Taylor explained.

The bus pulled up and they all began to get on. "Anna, that coat is so beautiful," Taylor said, staring in awe as she got on.

"Oh, thanks, babe," Anna said, laughing. "Guess where I got it?"

"Where?"

"Cromwell Gilly made it for me. He did a photo-shoot for his portfolio last week, and this was one of his designs. He let me buy it off him."

They all stared at it. "So pretty," Kaitlyn whispered in adoration. It really was a magnificent coat, and it fit Anna to perfection.

"I think I'm going to ask Cromwell Gilly to make me my grad dress," Anna said, considering.

"Grad? But that isn't till next year," Alexandra said in disbelief. "Why are you planning it so early?"

Anna shrugged. "Why not? It's grad."

Alexandra shook her head. "I haven't even thought about grad yet. Besides," she added pointedly, "the academy almost always has rehearsal during prom. I guess that doesn't affect you though ..."

Everyone looked up and stared at Alexandra. "What do you mean?" They looked back at Anna.

Anna smiled. "I think what Alexandra's being sweet

enough to mention is that I am not going to be at the academy next year. I wanted to keep it a secret, but —" she shrugged and looked at Alexandra.

"That was low," Grace whispered to Alexandra, glaring at her. "You knew that she didn't want anyone to know."

"But Anna, why?" Tristan asked. He sounded close to tears. "You've been going to the academy as long as I have!"

"I know," Anna sighed. "It's been a difficult decision, but I just really wanted to make my grade twelve year a good one, you know?"

"So this is for sure?" Jessica said in disbelief. "You aren't going to be here next year?"

"Actually," Anna said, "I'm not going to be here in a few weeks." She giggled.

"What?" Tristan half-screamed. "What do you mean?"

"My parents don't think I should dance at the academy if I am going to leave anyway." Anna shrugged. "The high school I used to go to in West Van runs on a semester system, so I'm just going to go there, and then I can take class at my old dance school."

"But why?" Tristan wailed. "I thought you wanted to be a ballet dancer!"

"Yeah," Alexandra agreed. "How do you expect to get any better if you leave the academy?"

Anna's perfectly arched eyebrows popped up and she smiled, showing her dimples. "I don't want to be a ballet dancer," she said simply. "I love dance, but you don't make any money dancing. I don't want to do it for the rest of my life." She shrugged and turned back to her lunch.

Kaitlyn stared at Anna. It was as though a basic tenet of her life had been disproved. *What did she mean that she didn't want to be a ballet dancer? How could she not?*

The bus pulled up to the academy and they all tumbled out, still thinking of things that they needed to ask Anna. "Anna, Anna," Taylor said, talking to her unafraid now that she knew she was leaving the academy, "do the Demidovskis know that you're leaving?"

Anna shrugged. "I think my parents told them," she said unconcernedly.

Out of them all, only Julian seemed unsurprised, aside from Grace and Alexandra, of course. Kaitlyn eyed him suspiciously, and then dropped back to talk to him. "Did you know about this?" Kaitlyn whispered.

Julian shrugged. "She didn't tell me," he said. "But I thought it was pretty obvious that she was going to quit. Come on, she went on vacation instead of doing a *pas de deux* with Tristan, and she didn't even register for YAGP." Kaitlyn followed Julian into the hallway, confused as to how someone as clueless as Julian could have noticed something that she didn't. It had just never occurred to her that someone at the academy might quit, at least someone that was doing well. Now, if it had been Angela who had quit, that would have made sense …

After class, Kaitlyn avoided looking at Taylor, who kept unsubtly signalling her to hurry up. She got changed into her jeans and American Eagle T-shirt, took down her bun and attempted to brush out her hair, pulled her wet socks onto her sweaty feet, then put on her boots and her coat, and slung her bag over her shoulder. "Okay, I'm ready."

"Omigod, finally!" Taylor exclaimed. "That took so long!"

"Uh, it took, like, seven minutes," Kaitlyn protested, looking at her cellphone. She followed Taylor and Keiko upstairs.

"Now, go round to my mom," Taylor ordered, "and I'll trick Julian into coming around."

"Okay." Kaitlyn and Keiko exited by the side door as Taylor intercepted Tristan and Julian coming up the stairs.

Charlize was waiting in the car, and she unlocked the doors so that Kaitlyn and Keiko could get in. "Taylor coming?" she asked.

Keiko nodded. "She's just getting Julian and Tristan," she explained. They sat in the car. A minute went by, and then another — Charlize looked at the clock. "Where are they?"

Keiko and Kaitlyn were silent. Kaitlyn could feel the sweat from her body going through her shirt. *Gross.* She pulled it away from her torso and shifted in the seat. She looked out; *oh.* "There's Taylor," she said as Taylor came around the building. "And Julian and Tristan, and … Alexandra."

Charlize frowned, looking out. "She's not coming, is she?" Charlize asked, referring to Alexandra. "I told Taylor only four people!"

They drew close to the car, and Taylor got in the front. She looked upset. "Taylor," Charlize hissed quietly. "I told you only four people! Alexandra isn't coming, is she?"

"Tristan invited her!" Taylor said.

"There aren't even enough seats!" Charlize got out of the car, smiling. "Happy birthday, Jules! Now, who's coming with me?"

"Everyone?" Tristan said.

"Oh, I see. I was not expecting this many people!" Charlize laughed in an extremely unamused way. "Well, I guess we'll have to see what we can do ..."

"It's fine," Alexandra said, following Tristan into the small car. "I'll just sit on Tristan's lap." In a few seconds everyone was in the car except Charlize. Charlize sighed and got in. She started up the car and began to drive away from the academy, unusually slowly. "I really hope we don't run into a police car," she said pointedly.

At Taylor's house, there were still Christmas tree lights up. "I keep meaning to get to it," Charlize explained as they got out, "but I never remember except when I am driving away or coming home and too tired to do anything about it.

Taylor rolled her eyes. "You always complain about being tired."

"Well, maybe I *am* tired, Taylor. A little gratitude would go a long way!" Charlize laughed and shook her head, but no one else laughed with her. It wasn't really that funny.

Taylor ignored her mother and led them all down to the side door. They cut through the wet lawn and went in. "This is my room," Taylor said, ushering them into an explosion of colour.

"Wow!" Julian said, impressed. "This bed is huge! And so bright!" He jumped up onto it with a flying leap.

"Agh!" Taylor protested.

"What?" Julian asked, sitting more sedately in a cross-legged position. "Do you never jump on it?"

"No, I don't," Taylor lied. "That ruins the springs."

Julian held his arms out as he sat in the centre of the bed. "Om ..." he intoned with his eyes shut. His eyes snapped open again, and he grinned. "This is awesome. It's like a magic carpet."

"That's nice, Julian," Kaitlyn laughed. "Are you Aladdin or Jasmine right now?"

"Neither," Julian said, his back stiffening with false dignity. "I am the great Julian Reese. You may have heard of me before now."

Taylor was bored, and annoyed. This was not how the party was supposed to go; it was supposed to go exactly as she wanted it to. "Is anyone hungry?"

"Yeah." Julian jumped off the bed.

They went upstairs and congregated in the kitchen. Charlize looked at them. "Hungry?" she guessed.

They nodded.

"All right, take some chips and wait until I'm ready," Charlize said. She poured two types in two large bowls, and they went downstairs again. Kaitlyn hopped down each stair. She felt strangely excited; it had been so long since she had actually just hung out at someone's house. It was awesome. Better than awesome; it felt like she was back in elementary school again.

"What do you guys want to do?" Taylor said. Julian

was lying on his belly, flipping through her DVDs. "*Tangled*, *Clueless*, *Mean Girls*, *Borat*, *Gossip Girl* — oh, cool, K-Ballet!" He sat up, pulling out *Swan Lake*.

Alexandra came over to look over his shoulder. "K-Ballet?"

"K-Ballet's in Japan," Keiko said, taking the case from Julian and looking at the back. "It is Tetsuya Kumakawa's ballet company. It is so good and so expensive to buy tickets to in Japan. Kageki tells me that Tetsuya dates many girls, but I love him, anyway."

Julian took the case back from her. "Can we watch this?" he asked, turning to Taylor, excited.

"Yeah," Taylor said unenthusiastically. "It's your birthday — or we could play a game or something."

"Let's watch this," Alexandra said firmly. They all trekked to the living room, and Alison snuck in to watch with them.

"Alison, go away, these are *my* friends," Taylor said, annoyed.

"Hey, Ali," Julian said, grinning at her. "Want to come and watch ballet?" He patted the space on the couch next to him.

"Yes." Alison hopped up beside him. Taylor pressed Play, and they all managed to fit on the couch.

"Where did you get this DVD, Tay?" Tristan asked curiously.

"Mao," Taylor answered. She took a chip and popped it in her mouth. Kaitlyn did the same. She wondered what would happen if she just ate exactly what Taylor ate for a couple of months. Would she lose weight, or just puff up like a blowfish from eating so much junk food? Taylor took another chip, and Kaitlyn mirrored her.

Julian was leaning forward, watching. "That person's not Japanese," he said, pointing at Prince Seigfreid's friend, Benno.

Keiko nodded. "He's from the Royal Ballet. I forget his name. But that is where Tetsuya trained and used to dance."

"Didn't they used to call him Teddy there?" Alexandra asked, turning around.

"I don't know. You know K-Ballet?"

"Of course," Alexandra said, smiling. "Aiko showed me them last year."

"Shush," Julian said. "You guys be quiet. Me and Alison are trying to watch the movie." They all stopped talking and focused back on the screen.

"I love that ending," Julian said wistfully as the movie finished. "It's so perfect … I think more companies should have that ending. I hate how Odette and Seigfried or one of them just die usually. That heaven scene was sweeeeet. I liked how they used the gauzy curtain, too."

Taylor turned on the lamp, and suddenly they could see. It had gotten dark outside while they were watching, and there was no longer any light from the big window. "Tristan, are you crying?" she exclaimed.

"No," he protested, dabbing his eyes. Alexandra passed him a Kleenex from her pocket and blew her own nose.

"You guys are silly," Keiko said, shaking her head. "It is just a story. Very tragic, but a story."

"I know that," Tristan said indignantly.

"Guys, are you done with the movie?" Charlize asked, coming into the living room. "Oh, good. Come and eat."

They slowly got up. "I just want cake," Taylor said. "I don't want dinner."

"Me, too," Julian said, yawning as he stretched.

Alexandra shrugged. "I don't care — I'd eat cake over dinner."

"Taylor!" Charlize sighed. "Look what you started, and I just spent all this time making dinner."

"Oh, I'm so sorry, Charlize," Julian said quickly. "Of course we'll eat dinner. We were just excited for cake."

"Can we just have cake? Please Mom, nobody even wants dinner."

Kaitlyn's stomach rumbled, and she covered it with her hand.

"Okay, what is going to happen is you can all come to the table, and the people that want cake can have cake, and the people that want dinner can have dinner," Charlize said firmly. "Come on."

They went into the dining room, and Kaitlyn sat down next to Taylor. Charlize had gotten an ice cream cake, and she brought it out, with seventeen sparklers on it. "Can I light it? Tristan asked.

"Sure." Charlize handed him the matches.

"You're old now, Julian," Taylor giggled.

"Whatever." Julian stuck out his tongue at her.

They got their pieces of cake, and Kaitlyn started to eat hers slowly. She looked over at Taylor: she was smooshing bits of the cake against her plate so that the cold, hard ice cream softened. Kaitlyn did the same, trying to match the amounts she ate with Taylor. The phone rang, and Charlize went to answer it. "Oh, hi, Cecelia."

Kaitlyn looked up. What did her mother want now?

"Of course, I'll hand you over to her right now." Charlize handed Kaitlyn the phone.

"Hi, Mom, what's wrong?"

"Nothing's wrong," Cecelia answered, her shaky voice revealing the opposite. "Kaitlyn, I was wondering if you could just come home? I need to talk to you."

"Mom, what's wrong?"

"Nothing's wrong, I just want to talk to you about something."

"Well, if nothing's wrong, I want to stay." Kaitlyn was suddenly very conscious of the others listening in close to her.

"Kaitlyn, I need you to come home."

"I'll come home in the morning, okay?" Kaitlyn hung up.

"Is everything all right?" Charlize asked politely. "Do you need to be driven home?"

"No, it's fine," Kaitlyn said, quickly. "My mom just wanted to make sure that I had done my homework."

"Are you sure?" Charlize was insistent. "I don't want to get in trouble with your mother if she wants you home."

Kaitlyn looked over at the table, where the others were watching. Nobody seemed disappointed at the idea that she might leave. At her seat, Kaitlyn could see her cake forming a chocolate puddle on the plate as her smooshed ice cream started to melt. "No, it's fine, actually," she said quickly. She sat down and began to eat her cake, spooning up the melted pool first.

"Do you remember when we put that chocolate ice cream under your bed in the dorm at NBS?" Alexandra asked suddenly, turning to Tristan.

Tristan started to giggle. "That was hilarious. That summer was so much fun." He turned to Julian, explaining the story. "We went on this field trip, and we really, really wanted chocolate ice cream, I don't know why — we were like, eleven years old."

"It was that time we both went to the National Ballet School for summer school," Alexandra interjected, noticing that Julian looked a bit confused.

"We got this big tub of it," Tristan explained, "because there wasn't anything else — and then we stuck it under our bed because we were called away. We thought we'd only be gone a few minutes, but it was at least two hours, and when we came back there was this gross chocolate lake under the bed. There must have been a hole in the tub."

"And then you left it!" Alexandra said indignantly, still horrified even after almost six years. "It was so disgusting. I don't even remember who cleaned it up, but it wasn't you."

"You should have cleaned it up, it was your fault."

"Nuh-uh."

Kaitlyn looked at Taylor as Alexandra and Tristan continued to reminiscence for Julian's entertainment. She looked very unimpressed, and kept opening her mouth to say something, but she didn't do it forcefully enough to interrupt Alexandra and Tristan's flow. Kaitlyn felt happy knowing that the birthday party that Taylor had been bragging about for weeks was not going as she wanted it.

The phone rang again, and Kaitlyn could hear Charlize answer it in the kitchen. "Oh, hi again!" she heard her say. "Oh yes, they're all just eating cake right now — do you want to talk to her?" There was a pause as Charlize listened. "I could just drive her home if you want Cecelia," Charlize said. Alexandra and Tristan had stopped talking to eavesdrop.

"What's wrong with your mother?" Alexandra looked down the table at Kaitlyn. Kaitlyn shrugged, feeling her face heat up with a blush.

"Let's all go downstairs," Taylor said quickly, taking advantage of the silence. She hopped up, leaving the plates behind her.

Julian started to stack the plates, and Alexandra and Tristan quickly joined in to help.

"Guys, you can just leave that. My mother won't care," Taylor said impatiently.

"Shush," Tristan said, annoyed. In the kitchen they could hear Charlize still talking on the phone to Kaitlyn's mother. "Oh, God, yes!" Charlize exclaimed, laughing. "I had exactly the same conversation with her last week."

Apparently they had moved on from discussing Kaitlyn to gossiping. Kaitlyn hoped that was the end of it, and that her mother had gotten over whatever had been bothering her. They started to bring the plates into the kitchen, and Kaitlyn swiped a decorative chocolate swirl off of the cake and into her mouth before she followed them.

"Kaitlyn," Charlize said as she walked into the room, "would you talk to your mother for a moment?"

Kaitlyn reluctantly took the phone from her as everyone else slowly headed downstairs, listening in. "Hey."

"Kaitlyn, I need you to come home," Cecelia said on the other end. Kaitlyn could tell that her mother was putting a lot of effort into forcing her voice to remain calm.

"Why?" Kaitlyn was trying to sound polite for the benefit of the curious ears listening in.

Cecelia lost her calm. "Kaitlyn, I understand this is important to you at the moment, but I need to talk to you."

"What about?" Kaitlyn hoped that nobody could hear her mother's voice through the phone.

"I don't think that you should go to competition."

"What?" Kaitlyn stared blankly out at Charlize's kitchen. It was very white, and the energy-saving fluorescent lights made the appliances and furniture gleam in such a way that it was hard for her to focus. "What do you mean?"

"Kaitlyn, I've been talking to Mr. Moretti, and looking at old competition videos — I just don't think that you are ready. I think you need to wait. There's no point in going if you aren't going to win, and I don't think that you are going to win."

"But ..." Kaitlyn didn't know what to say. "But, Mom ..." Kaitlyn couldn't say anything over the phone that she wanted to say, not with everyone listening in. *I'm doing much better, and I'm already signed up, and I really want to go. I have to go!*

"No, you don't have to go, Kaitlyn, we can say something. You should think about it. I think you shouldn't go. I want you to wait until we're sure that you are going to win."

Kaitlyn bit her lip. *She's already decided. But I can't not go! Everyone's expecting me to. I've been rehearsing for weeks ...* "Okay," she said to get off the phone. "I'll ... talk to you later? In the morning?"

Cecelia sighed on the other end. "Fine."

Kaitlyn passed the phone back to Charlize and turned to the stairs where the others were hanging at the bottom, listening in. Taylor had had enough. "Everybody, let's go upstairs now," she said, making an attempt to sound firm, but only succeeding in sounding annoyed.

"What was that about?" Tristan ignored Taylor, focusing on Kaitlyn.

"Um ..." Kaitlyn thought for a moment before the lie came to her, quite simply. "My mom thought that I hadn't done my science homework yet. She's a teacher, so she freaks out about that stuff."

"Oh."

"Come on, let's go to my room," Taylor said impatiently. They all started to walk upstairs, Kaitlyn last. *That was easy,* she thought. *They believed me.*

Chapter Eleven

Julian Reese

Can't. Get. La Bayadere music out of my head.

"Yes, that's it!" Theresa exclaimed. "So much better, Julian. Taylor, your arms are still extremely stiff. Your back doesn't move when you reach. Reach with your arms, feel your back stretch away in two directions — and *port de bras* down. Lengthen. Yes! You need to use every bit of your back. All right, now let's work on your solo Julian."

Julian nodded, panting, still not ready to speak. He stood up and moved to the centre of the room and began preparing. Just as Theresa was about to push Play, the door opened slightly. "Hey," Charlize said in her brightest voice.

"Hey," Theresa said right back at her, smiling also. It was painfully obvious that she was imitating her, but Charlize ignored it.

"I was wondering if I could just watch for a bit? See how it's coming along."

Theresa frowned. She did not want parents watching, but Charlize was already walking in and heading to the chairs. "I really feel that they can concentrate better if you are not in the room …"

"They won't even notice I'm here," Charlize winked at Taylor and Julian. "Right, guys?"

"Fine," Theresa snapped, unimpressed. "Julian, you ready?"

Julian nodded.

"Okay, then." Theresa pushed Play, and Julian started to go through his variation. He was still doing the solo from *La Bayadere*. He felt a bit better about it than he had at festival. His jumps felt higher, his turns cleaner, his knowledge of what moments to find in the music were better. But he also felt more nervous. Before festival, he had this feeling that it didn't really count, that it wasn't the important competition, and that he would do fine automatically. Because festival had come first, he hadn't had to think about YAGP. Now he did; now it was coming closer and closer. He felt like every time he did this solo he found another thing that he was doing wrong.

He finished with a flourish, and grinned. "Sorry, messed up the landing again," he apologized to Theresa.

"Don't apologize," she told him. "Fix it, but never apologize. It is your work, your art, not mine."

Julian nodded.

"Let's try it again. What I want you to do is focus on your feet; you are letting them fly about. If you stretch your feet, your legs will follow. You really need to concentrate on this, for everything."

Julian nodded.

"Have your teachers told you to work on this? It's your biggest problem right now."

"No," Julian said. "I don't think so."

Charlize coughed, bored.

Theresa ignored her. "Do it one more time," she told Julian. He nodded and ran to the side of the room, preparing with his hands inward toward his heart, hiding behind imaginary stage wings with his back to the audience. Theresa waited a moment. "Take your time with it, Julian," she said. "I know it feels like you don't have enough time, but you do, you have to just make the time. Breathe." She pushed Play, and Julian started walking on, leaping as the first few motes of the music started. He really, truly, loved this variation. It was just so dramatic and joyful at the same time. It didn't have any technical tricks that he was too terrified of doing, and it was short, and he loved the music.

"Good job," Theresa said as he finished.

"Thanks," he panted. The solo was short but exhausting. He pulled his wet shirt away from his skin and shook it to let in some of the moist warm studio air.

"Julian," Theresa said slowly. "You really do have something special, you know that, right? Other dancers, they might have stronger technique, or more tricks, but you have the heart. That is your strength. Don't ever forget to use that. Remember why you dance."

Julian nodded. For some reason he felt uncomfortable about Theresa praising him in front of Charlize. Charlize had started swinging her leather-clad foot in an annoyed manner. *Up, and down ...*

"What do you think?" Theresa asked, turning around fast enough to catch Charlize yawning.

"Oh, it looks good," Charlize said. "How is their *pas de deux* coming along?"

"Very good," Theresa said. "They're definitely improving. Now, do you want to see anything else? Because I feel that I can really coach them best with some privacy."

"Well, I would like to see my daughter dance," Charlize said pointedly. "This is a shared private, right?"

"Fine, of course, of course, Taylor, dear, come and do your solo."

Taylor nodded, walking away from the wall and toward the corner. She was doing Kitri's variation from Act 1.

"Now, remember, Taylor, it's about the flavour," Theresa said nervously. "Kitri has attitude, she has fire. Okay?"

Taylor nodded, biting her lip. She was obviously nervous to do her solo. *Which makes sense*, Julian thought. In the last three privates she'd had with Theresa, Theresa hadn't rehearsed Taylor's solo once, opting to work on their *pas de deux* and Julian's solo instead. *I wonder if Taylor tattled to her mom? I bet she did, that's probably why Charlize came to watch today.*

She began her solo a bit late, and Theresa stopped the music. "Again," she said. "Take a breath, dear."

Taylor nodded, and took a melodramatically big breath, puffing out her cheeks and then letting the air out in a shuddering gasp. She shook out her arms and legs and then stepped into position once more. "Okay, I'm ready now."

"Okay." Theresa pushed Play again, and this time Taylor was on time until about halfway through the solo, at which point she got behind, and then in trying to catch up, got ahead.

Taylor finished in a giggling mess. "Oops," she said. Theresa looked utterly unimpressed. Charlize looked upset.

"We have mostly been working on their *pas de deux*," Theresa explained, turning to Charlize. "Apparently she hasn't been improving with her own practice — Taylor, have you been practising at home?"

Taylor nodded. Charlize swung her foot violently, and the motion forced Theresa to look over at her. "But I'm not paying you so that she can practice at home," Charlize said sweetly. "Taylor needs to know what she has to work on. That's why we come to you."

"Of course," Theresa said, getting flustered and annoyed. "But we need to rehearse everything."

"Including her solo."

"Of course, of course. Now that we know it needs work we can spend more time on it next week."

"Next week is very close to competition time — maybe you could give her something to work on now?"

"Yes, yes, let me see," Theresa twisted her hands, nervous and put on the spot. "Julian, what do you think she should work on? You're good at critiquing others."

Julian started. He'd been zoning out. "What?" *What, she wants me to correct Taylor? Oh geez, this is going to make Charlize furious ...* "Um, maybe you could work on your timing, Taylor? And control the landings of your jumps more?"

Taylor nodded, not listening. She was busy looking

at her mother, who would have had steam and shooting fire around her head if she had been a cartoon character.

Theresa looked at the clock. "Oh, look, it's time!"

"Do you mind if I talk to you a minute?" Charlize asked, standing up.

"Of course," Theresa agreed, clearly meaning anything but. "I have a meeting, though, so it will have to be quick."

"Go get changed," Charlize ordered Taylor and Julian. They obeyed, walking out of the room as slowly as they could, hoping to hear something.

"I am not paying for privates so that my daughter can watch Julian rehearse —" Charlize said as Taylor closed the door behind them.

Julian was worried as they went downstairs. "I hope your mom isn't mean to Theresa," he said.

"My mom isn't mean!"

"I know, it's just Theresa didn't mean anything by not rehearsing your solos. She's just been busy working on our *pas de deux*."

Taylor didn't comment.

"What? You don't think she meant anything by it, do you?"

Taylor shrugged. "Do you have your hotel booked?"

"Yeah. Me and Tristan are going to be sharing a room. You staying with your mother?"

"Yeah. Should be so much fun." Taylor sighed. "She is so annoying to travel with. Are your parents coming?"

"No."

"Did you ask them to?"

"No, they know when it is, but I don't really care if they come or not, so I just didn't ask them. It's a lot of money."

"Yeah. I wish I could make my mom stay home and not watch. That would be cool."

"Your mom's nice. She really cares about the stuff you do."

"I'd rather have cool parents like yours. They let you do whatever you want! Me, if I'm like half an hour late I get in so much trouble, and you could probably disappear for weeks and your parents wouldn't care."

Julian shrugged. "Yeah, but then again, they also don't drive me everywhere, and plan my life for me, and help me with my homework."

"I'd still take your parents over my mom any day. My dad's cool, but my mom's so annoying. She just doesn't get that it's my life."

"Is your dad coming?" Julian asked to change the subject. "He lives in the States, right?"

"Yeah, he lives in L.A., but he can't come — he has a business trip."

"Oh." Julian bit his lip. Taylor really liked her dad and thought he was super cool — he was a talent agent in California, and she talked about everything he did like he was perfect, but Julian thought he sounded like a bit of a douche. He also didn't seem to care nearly as much about Taylor as she thought he did. When she had told him that she was considering dropping out of school, he had told her to follow her heart, which Taylor had taken to mean that he was supportive, but Julian thought that it more showed that he just really didn't care. Charlize seemed nuts at times, but she also seemed to genuinely care about what Taylor did and was always trying to force her to do things that she thought would help her.

"Julian!" Julian turned around. Cromwell Gilly was waving at him from the door of the change room.

"Hey." He walked over. "What's up?""

"I found a different costume for you to wear for your variation," he said excitedly. "Come here."

Julian followed Cromwell Gilly into the costume room. It was protected by a large fire-resistant door, and resembled a dungeon, if there was a type of dungeon that had walls lined with ancient, sweaty-smelling tutus and fake flowers. Julian picked up a fairy wand and began rapping the shelves with it as he passed them by. He always felt a bit nervous walking in this place; it was cramped and underground, so it had no windows, and it reminded Julian of an Edgar Allen Poe story he had read when he was a kid. He couldn't really remember the names of the characters or anything had happened, he just remembered that some guy had accidentally walled himself up in a dungeon while trying to wall another man up. Julian shivered.

"Stop that," Cromwell Gilly said, annoyed. He walked backwards and snatched the wand out of Julian's hand. "Come on. Don't touch anything."

They got to the back of the costume room, and Cromwell Gilly took down a hanger. "Here. Try this on."

Julian pulled the loose Arabian pants over his ballet shorts. The top elastic bit actually fit his hips, and the legs were the right length. "Cool! This fits so much better, Cromwell Gilly!"

"Good," Cromwell Gilly muttered, stepping back to look at it. "Yes it looks much better. Move about a bit."

Julian jumped up and down and flung his arms and legs about.

"Stop! Okay. Good. Now, try this on —" Cromwell Gilly handed him a matching vest.

Julian tried to pull it on. "It doesn't fit."

"That's because you haven't undone the hooks," Cromwell Gilly said with a sigh. Julian took the vest off his head and handed it over to Cromwell Gilly, who undid it and then handed it back to him.

"Now it does," Julian said, raising his arms as Cromwell Gilly did up the hooks for him. "It totally fits."

Cromwell Gilly laughed. "You idiot. Okay, I know it will work now, so take it off before you do something stupid and destroy it."

Julian took it off. "Did you just find it?" he asked. The costume that he had worn for festival had been the only one that Cromwell Gilly could find that remotely fit him.

"No," Cromwell Gilly said, delicately putting the costume back on its hanger. "Andrew Lui's mother just donated a bunch of costumes."

"What? I'm actually wearing one of Andrew Lui's old costumes?" Julian said excitedly.

"Yes." Cromwell Gilly smirked. "Go upstairs. To the landing by Studio A."

"Why?"

"Go look. There's a picture that you should see."

Julian frowned, confused. "What?" He ran out of the costume room and up the stairs, making a racket on the way up. He stopped at the landing, spinning around on his heel as he tried to see what Cromwell Gilly wanted him to see. *Pictures.* He walked around, looking at each one in turn as he tried to look for something that made sense. There was an old black-and-white of the Demidovskis dancing together when they were young, a signed poster from Vancouver Ballet, a recent picture of Leonie Camden alongside an article telling of her promotion to soloist, and *oh!* Julian looked closer at a photo of Andrew Lui in a *jeté. Those are totally the same pants!* Julian ran downstairs. "Thanks, Cromwell Gilly!" he called from the doorway of the costume room, not wanting to enter again. "I saw the picture! So cool!"

"Mmm," Cromwell replied from somewhere in the depths of the costume room. Julian left, running upstairs to get a space at *barre.* He could hear the increase in noise upstairs that meant that class was about to start.

After class, Julian sat down on the bench in the boys' change room, too exhausted to move. He wished that he could apparate home. He didn't want to get up and put on his clothes and go outside and wait for the bus in the cold, and get off and then walk another four blocks until he was finally home. He let his head hang down and his eyes close for a minute. He yawned. The cold front of his locker felt good against his back, which was loose and warm from the day's dancing.

"Julian."

"What?" Julian complained, opening his eyes slightly.

"Wake up."

"No."

"Okay, fine then, go to sleep here, I don't care." Tristan walked off, whistling the music to his *Sleeping Beauty* variation as he went to get changed.

Julian groaned and unhappily got up, pulling his jeans over his shorts because he was too tired to get fully changed. He fell back down to the bench again to put on his shoes.

"How's your contemporary *pas* going?" Tristan called from the sinks.

"Good," Julian answered.

"Who are you getting to coach it again?"

Julian pretended he didn't hear.

"Julian?"

"What? I'm going home now, see you tomorrow, 'kay?"

"'Kay."

Julian walked upstairs and down the hall. He could feel something hurt on his inner thigh; he had probably pulled it during class when Mr. Moretti had grabbed his leg and pushed it up toward his head.

"Julian," Taylor called. She was standing at the entranceway, still in her dance clothes.

"See ya," Julian called, waving.

"No, come here," she called. Julian fought the urge to run for the side door, mostly because he was too sore to run, and walked slowly over to her. "What?"

"Want to go upstairs and rehearse? We haven't gotten

to do our contemporary *pas* together at all this week."

"Um —" Julian ran his hand through his hair. He didn't really have a choice, it had to be done. "Okay." He followed Taylor upstairs, and took off his jeans and socks. At least he didn't have to go downstairs to get his ballet shoes. Taylor put the music into the player and pushed play. Julian massaged his leg, an expression of pain on his face. "Ow, ow, ow ..." The music, "Sail," by Awolnation, started to play, and Julian straightened up.

Charlize walked in. "Hey guys. Working hard?"

"We just started, Mom," Taylor said, annoyed. "Can you please push Play for us?"

"Okay." Charlize walked over, her heels making a clicking sound on the floor. Taylor walked over to the side of the stage with Julian. "Now?"

"Yes." The piece was highly energetic and dramatic, which suited them normally, but at the moment they were both so tired that they barely got through it. Charlize watched them with a frown. "Why don't you guys just work on pieces of it, instead?" she asked. "Like that *penche* you have at the end, Taylor, it's not quite reaching 180 degrees. Can you make it straighter?"

"Yes," Taylor said indignantly. She went into the *penche* and straightened up.

"It's not there yet," Charlize informed her. "It has to be higher."

Taylor pushed upward with her chest, held her supporting leg's hamstring until it felt like it was on fire, and pulled her working leg up farther with her back, butt, and leg.

"There, that was it, Taylor," Charlize said enthusiastically. "Julian, maybe you should work on that *attitude* turn you have? It isn't quite as steady as it probably should be."

Julian nodded and started to work on it. Funnily enough, his turns got better when he was tired ... he went around and around, his mind clearing of everything except for the pleasant feeling of turning into a human top.

After Charlize dropped Julian off at home, he went straight to the kitchen. His dinner was waiting for him on the table, and he sat down, eating it as fast as possible. He squirted some dish soap on the plate, ran some water over it, and sort of cleaned it off with the dish cloth, then stuffed it on the drying rack. He went into his room and collapsed on his bed, summoning just enough energy to take off his clothes, turn off his light, and crawl into bed. *Teeth? Crap. No teeth.* As he lay there under his covers, he felt a strange sort of peace. It was pleasant to be this tired, to know that he had done all that he should for the day. *Oh! Noooo ...* he moaned and rolled over, burying his head in the blissful blackness of his pillow. He'd forgotten to do his homework for math class. *I'll do it in the morning,* he told himself, reaching out and setting his alarm for half an hour earlier than normal.

Chapter Twelve

Alexandra Dunstan
Caaaaaaallllifornia!!! Mom can't stop playing the Beach Boys <3

There are a few things that some people plunge into with glee, which others view with abject horror. Some might find the idea of performing solo in front of a somewhat large audience undesirable, and avoid it at all costs. Add on to that scenario a situation where afterward you are judged on said performance, and most will have fled. Alexandra was not of their number. Alexandra was of the 1 percent, the percentage that lived for the stage and loved nothing better than squashing the hopes and dreams of others by proving that she was more worthy than they. So it was only natural that Alexandra was practically skipping as she danced through her house making sure that she had left nothing behind. It was nothing to her that it was 6:00 a.m.; she was wide awake and ready.

Justin was not so thrilled. Having been entrusted with the task of taking his mother and sister to the airport and was currently in the awkward position of trying to sleep on the small kitchen island as they gathered their stuff. "Are you ready yet?" he asked. Or, rather, moaned.

"Justin!" Alexandra shouted. "It's time to go!" Her sympathies did not extend far, and quite excluded her brother; therefore, the idea that the decibel level required to express her excitement might make her brother momentarily hate her did not cross her mind. Her mind was happy, in the blissful state that comes when someone is about to illustrate why they deserve a place on this earth. Existential angst was a disease that frequently troubled Alexandra, but YAGP had put this disease in remission. They went to the car and Justin turned the heat up full blast.

"Alexandra."

"Yes?" Alexandra turned to her mother.

"You are going to do beautifully. I can feel it."

"Thank you."

"No, thank you. I don't tell you enough, but you really do make me and your father proud."

Alexandra was not sure what to say. The words coming out of her mother's mouth were the polar opposite to the opinions she had been expressing in the last couple of weeks. At the wheel, Justin appeared to be thinking the same thing; and he snorted. Snorting he could do at this hour.

Julian was barely awake as he followed Tristan up to the gate and set his suitcase on the conveyor belt. U.S. security guards never failed to make him nervous. In fact, the United States in general never failed to make him nervous. He thought of the things that his parents and their friends babbled about, lack of freedoms and overreactions, and he smoothed his hair back with a sweaty palm.

"What are you worried about?" Tristan whispered as they collected their stuff on the other end of the belt, subject to the intimidating glare of the large woman who handed them back their shoes.

"I'm worried that they will think I'm a terrorist," Julian whispered back. This thought was not entirely what had been worrying him, but it seemed to give a clear shape to the otherwise formless fog of abstract fear that he was feeling.

"I am far more likely to be called a terrorist," Tristan whispered back, pointing at his face.

Tristan might have a point.

"You on the other hand," Tristan continued, "are more likely to be accused of trying to audition for One Direction."

"What is One Direction?"

"You are seriously living under a rock, Julian. Never mind, they're English," Tristan answered, unwilling to explain the finer details of his love for Louis Tomlinson.

Julian shrugged, confused.

They reached the waiting area, where Keiko and Taylor and her mother sat.

"Are Kaitlyn and Alexandra on this flight?" Julian asked.

"Alexandra should be here," Taylor answered. "Kaitlyn I think is going on a different flight — her aunt had air miles or something, but not on this plane."

"Right," Julian remembered. "She said something like that."

"Yes," Taylor nodded. "At the studio. Yesterday." She sat on the floor and began to stretch; casual conversation, at least of the linear kind, was quite impossible with the level of excitement in the air. Beside her, Keiko did the same.

Behind Julian, an elderly gentleman rapped him on the back with a rolled magazine. "Excuse me," he asked, "but what is going on?" He pointed to the curiously shaped tutu suitcases.

Julian laughed. "A dance competition," he explained. "Those are tutus."

The man raised his eyebrows so far he nearly raised his hat. "I see. I couldn't guess it, was thinking maybe music. Or the circus. Interesting." He walked off, and Julian got the definite impression that they had been the odd point of his day.

Alexandra arrived, panting and leading her mother by several metres. "Everyone ready?" she asked. "Where's Kaitlyn?

"She's going to be on a different flight," Taylor repeated, cracking the bones of her left foot through her shoes.

"How unique of her." Alexandra sat down and began to flip through their schedule. "Julian, I think I'm going to be able to watch you and Taylor's contemporary *pas de deux.*"

"Sweet," Julian said, blushing. He could feel the warmth fill his face. It was so annoying, he seemed to be entering his awkward pubescent age at seventeen, and he objected. He squished his hands against his hot cheeks, trying to restore them to his natural pale colouring.

"Did you —" Alexandra paused. She had been on the point of asking Julian a question that would have revealed that he had choreographed the *pas de deux*, and while she had no real commitment to keeping his secret, it did seem a bit tacky to blurt it out with him right there. He might stop telling her secrets if she did so. There was a moment of awkward silence as everyone looked up, the inevitable result of breaking off a sentence that hastily. They stared at each other, and suddenly Julian collapsed to the floor, giggling. "Oh, God."

"What?"

"You all know that I choreographed it."

They started to laugh. "We are so good at keeping secrets, Julian," Taylor said.

"You might as well have just posted a notice on the bulletin board in that case," Alexandra said dryly.

"At least the Demidovskis don't know I choreographed it," Julian shrugged.

Taylor looked up. "Uh, Jules, I heard Theresa telling them about it."

"Oh, God."

"Don't worry about it," Alexandra shrugged. "You have nothing to worry about if you're any good."

"Thanks, Alexandra, that really makes me feel better."

The hotel was packed with dancers, and as Taylor and Julian disappeared to rehearse, Alexandra stood in the middle of the lobby, digesting the scene. Tristan stood behind her, the two of them having made the decision to leave Beth and Tristan's mom Kaveri to gossip together. Alexandra needed air, and space, and this brightly lit hotel had neither. It smelled of central air and was filled with people hurrying around. There was an oddly stressed vibe in the hotel, and it was clear that YAGP was to blame.

"Alexandra!" Tristan pulled on her arm.

"What?"

"Look over there!" Tristan pointed, and Alexandra saw before them a very well-dressed pair. It is a wonderful sight when money meets taste, and Alexandra admired their clothing for a second. They were both of average height, with the same unusual combination of very tan skin and auburn hair paired with green eyes. They also had the muscle tone of exceptionally good dancers. Alexandra swallowed. "It's them! You know, I can't remember their names, remember you showed me their *pas de deux* on YouTube?"

Alexandra nodded, slowly. "Lux Amdahl. Lux and Nat Amdahl."

"Lexi, please introduce me? Please, please, please?"

"All right," Alexandra shrugged. "If she even remembers me — I only met Lux, and that was a while ago." They started to walk over, and before they had reached the pair, Lux had spotted Alexandra.

"Lexi! Omigod, you are here?"

"How are you?" Alexandra asked, smiling as she reached out to hug her.

"I'm good," Lux said, grinning. Alexandra watched her, a bit confused. The last time she had seen Lux, she'd been a spoiled but extremely talented eleven-year-old who had looked up to Alexandra. That had been two years ago, and Alexandra had a feeling things had changed. The spoiled brat had turned into a very determined-looking thirteen-year-old.

"This is Tristan, he goes to my school," Alexandra said, awkwardly pointing at him. Lux smiled at him. "Tristan, Lux. Well … I'm going for a walk. Do you want to come with?"

"Yeah," Lux agreed. "Omigod, so exciting, right? I can't wait to get on stage, and I love how so many people I know are here!" She pulled out her phone and began to text. The four of them began to walk toward the doors. Alexandra felt extraordinarily happy. She felt like she was home in this foreign hotel; she respected Nat and Lux, and that was an unbelievably freeing feeling. She hated the academy because she never knew what was going on, why they chose some people over others, why they loved Grace more than her. Here, she knew where she stood. Tomorrow she would be able to see if Lux was as good as she looked. She hung behind her, walking arm-in-arm with Tristan as he talked to Nat, and Lux strolled down the street ahead of them, too full of energy to wait. The skinny kid was still extremely skinny, but there was hard-core muscle on that body, and the hyperextension in her legs was something new. She listened absent-mindedly as Tristan and Nat argued about the point of competitions.

"I don't think that it should be like that," Tristan was

saying, sounding a bit unsure. "You shouldn't have to do competitions to get a job, because in a company you will have to dance completely differently. Competitions are kind of stupid, it's like they turn ballet into gymnastics or something. I'm just doing it because I'm Canadian, so I should do anything that I can put on my resume that will help me get a visa for the U.S. or wherever. If I just wanted to work in Canada, I wouldn't compete."

Nat snorted. It was a very obvious and kind of grown-up snort, and Alexandra could feel Tristan's arm tense. She squeezed his arm, reminding him not to be too rude; she wanted to hang out with Nat and Lux; they were definitely the most important and interesting people at competition this year.

"That is because you are a total competition virgin," Nat declared, "and you have been brainwashed into believing all the pretentious crap about competitions taking away the artistry. It's such total idiocy." They continued to argue for the rest of the walk, Tristan losing more ground with every step. He seemed to have had his feelings hurt by Nat suggesting that it was his lack of experience that made him think like he did, and as a consequence he was too emotional to formulate a logical argument. Alexandra didn't bother to help him; the truth was that she agreed with both sides.

Kaitlyn was currently sitting on a chair in her living room, worrying about what people must be thinking of her disappearance. The truth, that after the morning she had crossed nobody's mind, probably would not have reassured her, but was nothing compared to the conversations that were playing out in her mind. She bent her head down into her hands, massaging her forehead as if that could make her brain stop worrying.

"It's for the best, Kaitlyn," Cecelia said with a shrug, as she came out of the kitchen with a pile of her grade three students' math work to mark. "This way you won't be placed in a position where you will fail."

"Mom, nobody's going to believe that I got pneumonia."

"Yes, they are, Kaitlyn."

Kaitlyn sighed and turned on the TV. She might as well catch up with the latest episode of *Once Upon a Time*, since there was clearly nothing else to do. She felt so wrong; all that rehearsal, just to not dance. Logically, she knew that did not make sense, improving as a dancer was valuable all the time, not just for competitions and exams, but it felt horrible to put in that amount of work and then not get to go. She glared at her mother's back as Cecelia marked her students' work.

The rehearsal studio that Charlize had found for Taylor and Julian was painted pink and had posters with inspirational sayings and small girls in floppy tutus putting on *pointe* shoes covering the walls. In the corner was an ancient CD player, and next to it was a plastic bucket full of stuffed animals. Taylor giggled. "I miss dancing in places like this," she said.

"Uh-huh," said Charlize, her heels making a clicking noise as she walked across the floor to the cheap chair in the corner, sitting down and crossing her legs. "I don't miss you dancing in places like this. I don't want to be rude, but the mothers were a bunch of crazies." She found her lipstick in her purse and began reapplying it as Taylor and Julian warmed up and Theresa tried to figure out how the CD player worked.

In the end it was Charlize who managed to get the CD playing, and Taylor and Julian began to rehearse. Charlize couldn't help laughing as they finished even though she had seen them do it a million times. "Looks good," she said. "You guys look adorable."

Alexandra laid out her outfits in front of Lux, as the other girl sat on the bed, admiring them. "I like that tutu. Did you get it made in Vancouver?"

Alexandra nodded and changed the topic; Cromwell Gilly made tutus for *her*, she didn't want him to make tutus for Lux. "Your brother seemed a bit … passionate about competitions earlier. I think he kind of hurt Tristan's feelings."

Lux shrugged. "That's just Nat. He doesn't mean to be rude. It just happens. Tristan should be less sensitive, Nat was only having fun."

"Oh." Alexandra began to fold her contemporary leotard, keeping her opinions to herself. As far as she was concerned, Nat's comment to Tristan about him being a competition virgin, had been entirely meant and calculated to hurt. It had made her slightly angry as she believed that she was the only one allowed to be rude to Tristan. Tristan was partly right, anyway, international competitions were pointless most of the time when you were younger, except as practice; you weren't going to be looking for a job then. "So, what are you going to be doing when he goes to the Royal Ballet School in the fall?"

Lux shrugged. "It isn't even decided that he will go to RBS — he made it sound that way, but it isn't. I really have no idea. I guess I'll wait until after competitions." Lux looked at her foot, moving her big toe up and down out of her shoes, trying to air out her blister. "I'm going crazy. Gonna go find Nat and see if we can rehearse somewhere. Nice seeing you."

With that, Lux disappeared out the door. *Lux is possibly the most hyperactive person I have ever met.* Alexandra put her shoes down and went to shower.

As they walked into the hotel, Julian couldn't stop thinking about how nervous he was. The hotel was full of people who were obviously competitors, and Julian couldn't stop looking at them, trying to imagine what they danced like, how good they were. Taylor turned to him and gave him a quick hug. "See you tomorrow then?" she asked. "Unless you want to hang out with me and Keiko, I think we're gonna go to the pool before bed."

"No you aren't," Charlize said firmly. "You need some sleep, Taylor."

"I'll see you guys in the morning," Julian assured them, spotting Tristan across the lobby. He walked across, feeling extremely self-conscious. There were so many dancers, and even though logic told him that they probably didn't even notice him, emotion made him feel like they were watching and scrutinizing his every move. He finally reached Tristan's side. "What's up?" he asked. "Why are you behind here? Hiding from your mother?"

"No. Well, yes, but no." Tristan picked up his mug of tea and stood up, and he and Julian started heading to the elevator. "Guess who I just met?"

"Please say it was Joss Whedon."

"Who's that? And no, Nat and Lux Amdahl."

"Who are they?"

"Amazing. Lux and Nat Amdahl," Tristan said, with an air of explaining something to a not-too-bright child, "are both competing this year, at this competition, which means that Lux will probably win junior girl and Nat will almost certainly win senior boy. We don't have a hope because they are both brilliant. Nat is going to the Royal Ballet School in the fall." The elevator stopped and they both got off, walking down the hall until they reached the right room.

"RBS? That is so sick!"

"They're both amazing." Tristan inserted his door key, the green light flashed, and they went in. "I already called this bed." Tristan pointed at the bed near the window.

Julian shrugged and dumped his suitcase on the other one, pulling out his laptop. He checked his email — nothing from his dad. He hadn't heard from him since Christmas, and he wondered if he should be worried. He deleted a bunch of spam, and was about to delete one more when he noticed the subject line; *Satyagraha*. Apparently his mom's new email address was *childonarock@hotmail.com*. He opened it.

Hello dearest Julian,

I'm doing well, I feel like I'm in a good space. Busy busy busy as usual, you know me, I work too hard. That's the price of caring about other people too much – you neglect yourself. I've started training as an acupuncturist you'll be pleased to know, so that's been truly fascinating. If the West only ever woke up to the higher enlightenment that defines the East, I know we'd see magic happen.

Luigi and I have parted ways I'm afraid, I just couldn't deal with his materialistic mindset anymore. You know how it is. I'm too altruistic and sensitive and I hate it when people let themselves be tied down by greed. And his control issues! He wanted me to just be HIS with a capital H. I have to be free to experience *life*.

Anyway, Luigi won't be paying your homestay fees anymore – I understand you probably feel angry at him, babe, but

> Luigi has always been petty. So I suppose you'll have to let your father know you will be staying with him again.
>
> Be good to yourself.

Julian stared at the screen. *Crap.* Now what was he going to do? He couldn't go back to not dancing and staying with his dad, he would never be a dancer that way. *Why Satya? Why did you have to get rid of him before I graduated? Just one more year and a bit, that was it.* He'd liked Luigi, he was a nice quiet man, and he had been surprised and grateful when Luigi had offered to pay for his homestay bills. But then Luigi had probably thought he was the exception to Satya's swiftly rotating relationships, had thought that he would be in Julian's life for a long time. Satyagraha had a gift of making people feel like spending money the way she wanted them to. While she didn't particularly care if Julian went to the academy or stayed with his father, it would have pleased her for Luigi to pay her son's way.

"Is everything all right?" Tristan asked, stepping out of the bathroom and seeing Julian sitting there motionless.

Julian forced himself to look up and smile. "Yeah, of course."

"Cool," said Tristan, taking a flying leap onto his bed. "Let's see if there's anything on cartoon network. Oh look, Disney Channel reruns are on!

"I think I'm going to try and sleep," Julian said quietly. He got into his bed and pulled the covers over his head, but the temptation of Disney was too hard to resist and he poked his head out, watching, half-asleep as Selena Gomez tried to do magic. "Why is her brother so lame? If I could do magic I would be awesome."

Tristan laughed. "Yeah. You are also the dude that told me that if you ever choreographed a full-length ballet it would have samurai in it and it would be set to a combination of Radiohead, Coldplay, and Jakob Dylan."

"What's wrong with samurai?"

"Nothing. Nothing's wrong with samurai, just saying ..."

The morning started at 6:00 a.m. again for Alexandra. She needed to get up, feel her body moving to make sure that it felt right, that she was in control of it. She went to the small hotel fridge, took out a Happy Planet smoothie, and sat down on the bed to drink it and wake up. Today she could do anything — she hoped. She finished her juice and started to do the first parts of her hair and makeup.

Beth rolled out of bed, rubbing her eyes. "You up already, Alexandra?"

"Yeah."

"Want to go downstairs to get breakfast?"

"Okay." They quickly got ready and then went downstairs. Being alone with her mother felt weird for Alexandra. She wasn't quite sure what to say. She wished that Justin was there, too.

"Are you excited?" Beth asked. She seemed genuinely curious.

"Yes," Alexandra shrugged. "A bit nervous."

Beth shook her head. "I don't know how you can do this," she admitted. "I could never to up on stage and do what you do. I don't know how I gave birth to you and Emma."

Alexandra shrugged. "I don't really get scared," she said. "Just, worried if I don't feel like I am the best, or if I'm not ready. If everything's perfect, then it's so much fun."

Beth shrugged. "I didn't even like speaking up in class."

"This isn't like speaking up in class," Alexandra said impatiently. "It's completely different. It's telling a story, and it's awesome. I don't like talking in class, either." They walked down to the breakfast area.

"Are you feeling ready, then?" Beth asked.

"Yes," Alexandra said firmly. "I am. I think."

Taylor couldn't stop moving when they got to the theatre. Julian finally grabbed her by the shoulders and held her in one place. "Tay. Stop it. You're making me seasick."

"Okay, okay," Taylor agreed. The second he let go she began to hop up and down on the spot. "I'm so excited! I'm so excited! It's finally time!"

"Taylor, please save some of that energy for your dances?" Charlize requested. "Come on. Calm down and start doing your makeup."

"Okay, okay, okay." Taylor sat down in front of the mirror. "Can I put on blue eyeshadow?"

"No." Charlize sat down beside her. "Here. I'll do it." She began to expertly brush on the shades of brown and white eyeshadow.

Kaitlyn went online, staring at the YAGP website. There were pictures of previous winners scrolling on the top of the page,. She so badly wanted to be there. She just wanted to try to win. "Kaitlyn," Cecelia called from downstairs. "Come here."

Kaitlyn ignored her mother, clicking to the list of past winners. She knew most of them.

"Kaitlyn! What are you doing up there?"

"Coming," Kaitlyn answered, annoyed. She went downstairs.

"What were you doing?"

"Stuff."

"Well, I thought that you could start getting ready for your summer school auditions," Cecelia said impatiently. "Come on, you need to do something. You have just been moping about all day."

"I wanted to go," Kaitlyn muttered under her breath.

"What was that?"

"I said I wanted to go to competition!"

"No, you didn't," Cecelia said firmly, getting angry. "You agreed with me that it was best to stay home, because you were going to lose. Don't you dare say that to me now."

"Fine," Kaitlyn said. "I'm going up to my room." *I didn't say that. You tricked me into saying that.*

"Write down what you need for each audition, Kaitlyn. And the dates."

Kaitlyn walked up to her room and sat on her bed. It was so stupid; Mr. Moretti had kept changing what variation he wanted her to do every day, and now she couldn't go to competition. If he had just let her rehearse only the variation that she had wanted to do, she was sure that she would have won.

Julian was waiting in the wings beside Tristan. It was almost time for their solos. "You'll be okay," Tristan said, sounding worried. Julian realized that he must look as nervous as he felt.

"Yeah," he agreed. "It'll be fine. Fine, fine, fine ..."

"Just don't think about it as an audition or anything," Tristan advised him. "Just go out there and treat it like a show. All those people, they're just there to watch you, not to judge you. Okay?"

"Okay."

The bell rang, and a poised female voice announced: "Julian Reese, from Vancouver, Canada. Vancouver International Ballet Academy."

Julian ran on, smiling and looking not nervous at all. But then he stumbled on his first step.

"He's nervous," Kageki commented, standing next to Tristan.

"Yup," Tristan said, watching him worriedly.

"Does he go to your school?" Nat asked, stepping up behind them.

Tristan jumped. "Um, yeah. That's Julian."

Nat watched for a few minutes. "He's a bit shaky, isn't he? Oh dear. He just almost fell on that *pirouette*."

"He's good," Tristan said angrily. "He's just nervous. This is his first big competition."

"How old is he?" Nat asked, frowning.

"He just turned seventeen. Like me."

Nat sighed. "Look, I'm sorry that you got offended about me teasing you over having never done a big competition before, okay? I was just joking. I can be a bit harsh sometimes. I like to think that's part of my charm."

"Huh." Tristan turned back to the stage, watching Julian. Beside him, Kageki watched, looking back and forth between Nat and Tristan as he tried to figure out what they were talking about.

"Of course, if you're easily offended, I can understand why you'd be upset. My apologies."

"I don't think this is the time. I need to go over some stuff, sorry." Tristan walked over to the rosin box and rubbed some more into the bottoms of his shoes, and then began to test them out, *pirouetting* carelessly with his arms out to the side.

Nat followed him over. "Look, I'm sorry."

Tristan looked at him, considering. "Okay," he said suddenly. "But only because Alexandra showed me some clips of your variations at last year's competition and you were really good."

Nat laughed. "Okay. Valid."

* * *

Alexandra was waiting with Taylor and Keiko before their variations started, when she noticed that something was wrong. "Has anyone seen Kaitlyn yet?" she asked, worried.

"No," Taylor exclaimed.

"Me neither," Keiko agreed.

"Should we try and find out where she is?" Taylor asked.

"No," Alexandra answered. "There's no time. Look, they're about to start."

"I'll call her after I finish my variation," Taylor decided.

Alexandra nodded. She stepped out *en pointe*, practicing her *pique* turns. The place where her big toe rested in her right shoe suddenly felt a little soft, but there wasn't enough time to change shoes. It would be good for *pas de deux*, though; softer shoes were usually better for *pas de deux* work.

"Kaitlyn Wardle, Vancouver, Canada," the announcer called out. "*La grande pas classique*."

The man with a clipboard full of papers who was in charge of sorting all the dancers out backstage looked around. "Are either of you Kaitlyn?" he asked.

They shook their heads. "Kaitlyn doesn't seem to have showed," he said into his headset.

"Taylor Audley, Vancouver Canada," the announcer said after a pause. "Kitri, Act 1."

Taylor ran on, and Alexandra turned back to her own work, hearing the music in her head and going through everything that Mr. Demidovski had said to do in her privates.

* * *

After Taylor had finished, she ran outside to call Kaitlyn. She thought that she had done well, but it was hard to tell sometimes. She wasn't quite sure. It had felt good, she hadn't fallen, but who knew if it was what the judges wanted? She frowned; Kaitlyn wasn't picking up her phone. She pressed call again. And again. And again. She finally left a message; "Hey Kaitlyn, call me if you get this? We're worried about you … you just missed your variation. What happened? Call me back, babe. Kk, bye."

Julian walked out. "Time for our *pas de deux*," he said, grinning.

Taylor looked around for her mother; she wasn't around. "As soon as it's time for our contemporary *pas de deux*, I'm going to put some green eyeshadow on overtop," she said. "I think it will look awesome with my costume."

"I agree. Maybe you could do something else, too, like some abstract stuff on your face or something?"

"Help me when we finish our classical?"

"Yeah. Hey, where's Kaitlyn? I haven't seen her yet."

"I don't think she's here. She didn't go on for her solo."

"Oh, wow."

"Yeah. Come on, let's run it through once more, just marking it? I'm so nervous!" They began to dance the *pas de deux* on the concrete ground outside of the theatre, Taylor dancing with her huge warm-up boots over top of her *pointe* shoes so that the cement didn't ruin them.

* * *

Alexandra was getting changed into her contemporary costume when Lux came back, frantically undoing her bun to have it loose for her contemporary solo. She spotted Alexandra, and her face lit up. "Lexi, I watched your variation! You were so good!"

"Thanks," Alexandra said, half-sarcastically. She thought that Lux was just trying to be nice; she had been wobbly, and had almost fallen at one point.

"By the way, there's a slippery spot at —"

"Downstage right? Yeah, I found it."

"Me, too," Lux said, annoyed. "I nearly fell flat on my butt." She finished getting changed, and they both went backstage to mark out their solos. The curtain that separated the audience from the dancers was closed, and the stage was full of dancers marking out their solos (setting it to make sure that their solo fit the stage, using all the space). Alexandra started to go through hers, weaving through the other dancers with a determination that guaranteed her a clear path. With little warning, one of the backstage people started to come through, sprinkling Coca-Cola on the floor with apathetic abandon. As he passed, dancers jumped back to save their costumes from the Coke. *The downstage right corner, the downstage right corner*, Alexandra willed him. He got there and sprinkled liberally. Alexandra sighed in relief; now she didn't have to avoid that corner for her solo. The cola quickly dried, and the dancers began marking their work again.

* * *

Kaitlyn heard her phone ring and picked it up. The caller ID said Taylor Audley. She set it down again. The phone kept ringing, and she threw herself on her bed, giving up. She started to cry. It wasn't fair; she had rehearsed, she wanted to be there, she wanted to dance! She was better than Taylor, and stupid Taylor was there. Taylor was probably doing horribly. Kaitlyn was so much better. Her phone beeped, notifying her of a voice message. Kaitlyn ignored it, her face in her pillow. *At least I'm the youngest. I can go next year.*

Taylor waited in the wings with Julian, nervous, but not of performing; her fear over what her mother was going to say if she didn't like the new makeup she and Julian had painted on her face had managed to completely overtake the fear she had about going on stage. "It looks good, right?"

"It looks good," Julian reassured her. "Freaky, but in a good way. You might want to pull up your top a bit." Taylor pulled her top up so that less of her chest was showing and bit her lip. *It was Julian's idea, he thought it would look good*, she rehearsed in her head.

"Taylor Audley and Julian Reese, Vancouver, Canada. Performing 'Sail.'" They ran on, and Taylor stopped thinking of anything but the choreography. It was so fast, and the timing was so difficult to keep on top of, that she couldn't think of anything but what she was dancing.

Alexandra and Keiko had both finished all their dances. "Come on, let's go watch," Alexandra said to Keiko.

"Is it okay to leave our stuff?"

"Um … Let's bring it." Carrying their bags, they went into the audience. Alexandra headed toward Beth and then saw Tristan. She went over and dropped her bags down next to her mother. "I'm just going to sit next to Tristan, okay?" she whispered.

"No, you're not," Beth whispered back. "Sit down." She patted the seat next to her, and Alexandra sat down next to her mother. A few seconds later, Keiko and Tristan joined them. "You just missed Taylor and Julian," Beth muttered under her breath. "You said that Julian was choreographing their *pas de deux*, right?"

"Yeah, was it any good?"

"Good? Lexi, it was amazing. It would have been better with better dancers, but the choreography was incredible."

"Lux Amdahl and … Nat Amdahl, Hawaii, United States. 'Comfortably Numb.'"

"Don't you know them?" Beth whispered.

"Yes. Watch, Mom, they're really good." The music started to play, and Lux and Nat came on, Nat dressed entirely in black, and Lux in white."

Beside her Tristan was mildly hyperventilating. "That's Pink Floyd! They're dancing to Pink Floyd!"

Lux and Nat stood facing each other for a split second, their profiles to the audience, and then in a sudden motion, Lux stepped up onto *pointe*, *developing* her downstage leg *a la seconde*. She hit almost 160 degrees in less time than it would have taken Alexandra to *grande battement* her leg. Alexandra leaned forward, her mouth open. Lux and Nat were slightly scary when they danced together normally, but the combination of their intense personalities and the dark music that somebody rather wise had set their piece to, was frightening. The audience was quiet for a few moments after their *pas de deux*, and then suddenly they all started to clap, giving Lux and Nat the biggest round of applause of the night. Alexandra bit her lip.

Taylor and Julian were getting changed backstage when they heard the applause. "Uh, Julian," Taylor said, making a sad face as she took off her makeup; "I don't think that we won for contemporary."

"It's okay," Julian said. "Thanks for letting me choreograph it, Tay. It made this competition so much funner."

"So much more fun," Nat corrected as he followed his sister into the change room. She handed him his clothes from her bag and he left to the boys' change room to get changed. Lux began to get dressed as Taylor and Julian stared at her, rather rudely.

"Have I met you guys before?" Lux said finally, once all of them were changed.

"Ah, no," Julian and Taylor both said together, embarrassed. "I just go to the same school as Tristan," Julian said at the same time as Taylor said, "I dance with Alexandra."

"Oh," Lux nodded. "Small world. You going to the audience?"

"Yes," Taylor said quickly, and they followed Lux to the audience, leaving behind their stuff, still all scattered around the dressing room.

Kaitlyn finally picked up her phone again. She began to text Taylor;

"Hey, I'm really sick — I got pneumonia, and I couldn't go. Have you danced already? Tell me when you know who got what, okay?"

Taylor and Julian sat nervously next to Lux, who appeared to be completely relaxed. "How can you be so calm?" Julian asked her.

Lux shrugged. "There's nothing I can do now," she said logically. "I've danced how I've danced; now the judges are going to pick who they pick."

"They're probably going to pick you," Taylor wailed. "I'm going to go sit next to my mom. I'm way too nervous right now." She stood up and left, going to find Charlize.

* * *

Alexandra was so nervous that she couldn't speak. When she had finished her solo, she had felt confident that she was going to get something, but after watching Lux, she was no longer sure. "Calm down," Beth said, patting her hand. "You were good."

"But what if I don't win anything?" Alexandra whispered back.

"Then you'll try again next year. Breathe."

Taylor looked at her phone. "Taylor, what are you doing? Put that away," Charlize said beside her. "They're about start to announcing the winners." Charlize bit her long, pink, polished nails.

"It's Kaitlyn. She said that she has pneumonia," Taylor whispered back. "That's why she wasn't here."

Charlize frowned, taking her finger out of her mouth. "What? That is such a lie. I can't believe her mother — she just didn't take Kaitlyn because she was afraid she was going to lose like she did at Spring Seminar."

"Really?" Taylor considered. "Maybe."

"Tell her that I hope she gets better soon."

Taylor obediently texted Charlize's message, and a few seconds later got a response. "She says thanks, that was sweet of you."

"See?" Charlize said triumphantly. "People with pneumonia do not text back that fast, Taylor."

Taylor considered. "I guess not."

* * *

The adjudicators began to announce the names, and the dancers began to walk up, the names of all the dancers that didn't go to the academy meshing into a flow of nothing as they waited to catch their own names.

"Alexandra Dunstan. First place, Senior Classical Women's. Second place, Senior Contemporary Women's." Alexandra felt her body settle back into stability. She jumped out of her seat and walked quickly up to the stage to get her award.

"Taylor Audley, third place, Senior Contemporary Women's." Taylor ran up, nearly tripping on the stairs to the stage, and accepted her award, giggling the whole way.

"Keiko Sato, Top 10, Senior Classical Women's." Keiko went up and got her award, smiling and taking her time.

"Tristan Patel, second place Senior Classical Men's!" Tristan's mouth fell open and he had to be shoved out of his seat by Beth. Tristan quickly ran up, shocked that he had been beat only by Nat.

In the audience, Julian's smile had grown a little more fixed. He hadn't fully expected to win, but he hadn't expected to get nothing, either. He waited as each award was finally called, and there was nothing left. He sunk back into his seat, sitting alone; Lux had long since been called up. Lux and Nat got first place for *pas de deux*, and then Tristan and Alexandra. Julian sunk farther into his seat. *I don't even like competitions. Competitions are stupid, dance is an art, how can it be judged? I wonder what Mr. Demidovski is going to say about me not getting anything.*

"And finally, some special awards," the announcer said into the microphone. "The student awards are all donated, and take the form of scholarships, and we also recognize exceptional teacher coaching and choreography."

Julian considered ducking outside for a moment to gather his emotions before the rest all came back off stage; but the lights were on in the audience and he would have been too conspicuous.

"This year, we have three student awards; the Willow Award for Most Promising Contemporary Dancer; the Seger David Award for Most Improved contestant who has competed more than once; and the Gageton Family Award for Most Promising Classical Dancer." The announcer checked her notes again, seeming confused about something. "This year, the judges have combined the Willow Award with the Best Teacher Choreography Award." She paused. "Can I please have Julian Reese up here?" Julian stared blankly up at the stage for half a second, and then he ran up. The announcer looked at her sheet. "It says here that you choreographed both your solo and a *pas de deux*, and another student's solo?"

Julian nodded.

"Well! What a busy young man. Here you go." She handed him an envelope, and Julian ran to join the others, a huge grin lighting up his face.

Chapter Thirteen

Fan Page of Vancouver International Ballet Academy
Congratulations to our winners at YAGP! Alexandra Dunstan, Tristan Patel, Taylor Audley, and Julian Reese.

As soon as Taylor had stepped off the plane, she felt at home. The air was different, and the airport *looked* like Vancouver. She was the last one to get home because Charlize had wanted to stay in San Francisco for a few days; and she had managed to get a tan, at least on her arms and face! Outside it wasn't even raining, just cloudy. She followed Charlize and Alison to their car, and then suddenly remembered what she had meant to do as soon as she was back in Vancouver. She dug her cellphone out of her pocket and started calling Kaitlyn.

"Hey!" she said as Kaitlyn picked up.

"Taylor? What's up?"

"I'm back in Van now, just got off the plane. I just remembered, I forgot to tell you what everyone got!"

"Um, that's cool, like, everyone else told me, and the academy posted it on their website."

"Oh. Cool."

"Taylor, I'm actually in Science right now, the only reason I can talk to you is because Mrs. Flowers just went out to photocopy a handout."

"Oh, sorry — I, like, just wanted you to know I'm back. And you told me to tell you what everyone got and stuff."

"Aw, yeah, I did! You're so sweet! I'll see you at dance, okay?

"Is your pneumonia better now?"

"Yup. It's so sweet of you to ask, but I've got to go"

Taylor put her cellphone back in her pocket and slowly started to catch up to her mother and sister. It felt unbelievably good to get back. It had been fun to do nothing for a couple days in San Francisco, but she really wanted to go back to dance — plus, she wasn't going to miss all the walking Charlize had made her do in San Francisco. Who really wanted to see a prison anyway?

"Taylor! Hurry up!" Charlize called impatiently.

"Coming!" Taylor got in the car and closed the door. She suddenly grinned.

"What?" Charlize asked, driving out of the airport parking lot.

"I can't wait to start rehearsing *Coppelia*," Taylor admitted. "It's going to be the greatest, I'm so glad that I got cast as a Friend!" Taylor closed her eyes and leaned back against her seat, daydreaming. Except, in her dream she wasn't a Friend; she was dancing the lead, Swanhilda. She could picture it all, the pretty pink, brown, and cream dress she would wear, the flower headpiece in her hair. She hummed softly to herself as she danced the first act in her head. Eight perfect *pirouettes*, the audience was going crazy. Mr. Demidovski was standing up in the audience shouting "Brava!" *It's going to be so much fun starting rehearsal again.*

TAKE A SNEAK PEEK AT THE THIRD BALLET SCHOOL CONFIDENTIAL BOOK, *I FORGOT TO TELL YOU*

Alexandra Dunstan
Listening to Said the Whale, sewing pointe shoes, and done all my hmw. Life is good :)

There was a cool breeze blowing over English Bay. Alexandra stood at edge of the water, breathing in as she faced the wind. *Breathe. Breathe. Breathe.* She could feel her heart rate slowing down as the wind whipped around her face, cooling down her hot face. There. It was going to be all right, she was not going to let Grace win this time. She turned around and walked back toward the park behind the docks. She could already see Tristan and Julian there on the grass, and Grace; they were attracting a crowd around them. Apparently it was unusual to see people wearing ballet costumes in a park.

"Lexi, hurry up!" Grace called. "I'm cold! What are you doing?!" Alexandra sped up a bit, and as soon as she reached them began to unzip her hoodie and pull off her loose knitted pants, revealing her costume underneath.

"Sorry, just wanted to look at something on the water."

"Geez, can't you do that — I dunno, when I'm wearing clothes? I'm freezing here!"

"I'm sorry!"

Tristan silently reached out for her hand, and Alexandra stepped toward him on *pointe*, her foot on the makeshift wood sheet that had been placed on the grass for the occasion. She stepped into *arabesque*, and slowly bent into a *penche* as he reached for other hand.

"Good, good!" the photographer said, bouncing in his excitement. "This is really neat! Lots of interest here. You're really bendy, aren't you?"

Beside Alexandra and Tristan, Julian reached out for Grace's hand, but Grace didn't want to pose with him. She shoved his hands away.

"Alexandra!" she hissed.

Alexandra ignored her. "Let's do a lift next," she suggested to Tristan. He nodded.

"Alexandra!" Grace said louder, loud enough that the photographer could hear.

"Is there a problem?" the photographer asked, putting his camera down for a second.

"Not really," said Grace. "It's just Alexandra has forgotten that Tristan and I were supposed to paired together, and *she* was supposed to go with *Julian*, since Tristan and I are the first cast."

"Oh." The photographer scratched his head. "Uh, does it really matter? Because I'm really liking the photos I'm getting of these two." He looked at Alexandra and Tristan. "Hey, do you guys think it'd work if you could do something next to that tree over there? You boys grab that wood, and I'll start setting up the light. I think we could get something really mystical, really special, over here."

"Sure." Julian shrugged and started to help Tristan pick up the wood. Grace reached out and grabbed Alexandra's arm, gripping it so tight that it hurt. "Ow!" Alexandra said involuntarily. "Grace, let go of me."

Grace glared at her. "I think that *me* and Tristan should do the tree pose," she said loudly. "Since we are the first cast. And you and Julian are really only understudies."

Alexandra ignored her and followed the boys. They set the wood floor down on the grass, and the photographer carried on behind them, setting everything up around the tree and muttering to himself. Grace stepped onto the floor on the other side of Tristan and crossed her arms. "Tristan," she said sweetly, "I think we should do a lift. Want to do a fish?"

"No," said Tristan. "Not really. I don't want my face to be all red in the photo."

"Tristan!" Alexandra said suddenly, sounding excited. "Let's do that lift we were working on in *pas de deux* class yesterday, you know, the one where I'm in a backbend and you're holding me up? And then I can *port de bras* with my arms matching the trees, and it would look so sweet with the tree."

The photographer's face lit up. "That sounds exciting. Show me?"

Tristan and Alexandra went into their lift while Grace pouted at the side of them and Julian stood awkwardly on the grass, watching them.

"Maybe we could have your hair down?" the photographer suggested. "That way you'd look a bit like those woodland fairy things, what's the name, Greek Mythology ..."

"Dryads?" Alexandra suggested, smiling at him.

"Yes, those! I like you. Now, just take that elaborate hair watchimacallit out of your hair — I bet that took you a long time to do! Yes, now — don't bother brushing it, just a moment." He reached out and expertly separated the thick coil left over from Alexandra's bun into many little coiling strands and smoothed it off her face. "Perfect. I like how pale you are, it really works with the setting. Now, Tristan, if you could just do that thing you were doing before — yes, perfect, I love the expression on your face!" The photographer clicked around them as Tristan struggled to hold Alexandra in place. She could feel his wrist shaking slightly under her back as he held her. They dropped out of the lift far before the photographer had tired of taking shots of them, Alexandra bending forward to counteract the strain on her back and Tristan frantically shaking his wrist.

"My wrist's still sore from *pas de deux* class," he muttered to Alexandra.

"Aw, muffin," she answered flippantly, straightening up and cracking her back.

"Hate you."

"Love you."

"Aw, love you, too."

"Do you think you could go up and do that thing again?" the photographer asked. "I feel like we've got something really special here. I'm really liking this." He stepped away from the tree and looked out towards the ocean, trying to judge the light. "The light's going to start to go soon, so I'll try and hurry up."

Alexandra and Tristan nodded. "One, two, three," Tristan said quietly, and on the count, Alexandra jumped and Tristan lifted, and she was in the air again. Her dark brown hair flowed down her back, creating an archway over Tristan's head under the canopy of the willow tree.

"I think I have it," the photographer said, his voice hushed so as not to jinx it. He stared at the screen on his camera. "I think I've got exactly what I want here. Thanks, guys. You can put your clothes back on now." Tristan and Alexandra gratefully began to pull on their clothes. Alexandra began to shiver as she pulled on her sweatshirt, her cold body reacting with relief to its warmth. "You guys can go now," the photographer said, turning to Julian and Grace. "Sorry for having you come out for nothing."

Grace glared at him. He bent down and began putting his camera away, pretending that he couldn't see.

"Thanks," Alexandra said, smiling down at the photographer. "Want me to help you put the stuff away?"

"I got it," he said, looking up and smiling. "Thanks for making my job so easy. I love doing a shoot with dancers. You guys already know about positive and negative space, you create interesting shapes right away without me having to say anything. And don't get me started on that crazy stuff you can do with your body —" He let out a low whistle and turned back to his equipment.

"Thanks, that's so sweet of you to say!" Alexandra said. She walked over to Tristan and linked her arm through his. “Bye-bye, Jules, bye, Grace. See you at rehearsal tomorrow morning.” They began to walk down the Seawall, a long stretch of winding pavement with park on one side and the ocean on the other.

“Brrr, so cold,” Tristan said, shivering spastically to emphasize his point.

“Yeah.” Alexandra was busy thinking. “Do you think Mr. Demidovski will be upset with me that I was in the photo instead of Grace? I mean, they haven’t even decided yet if they are going to let me have a cast of Swanhilda.”

Tristan shrugged. He had gotten the role of Franz, and that was as far as his concern extended. “I dunno. Guess you’ll find out.”

Alexandra stepped away from his arm and onto the thick cement barrier between the ocean and the path. *Step, arabesque, step, arabesque.* She reached out suddenly for Tristan’s hand, grabbing it as she almost fell in the water. She hopped off the barrier.

“Tristan,” she said, as they continued along the path, “when we’re old and married, do you want to live in a house around here? Of course, we’ll be absolutely loaded then, too, so everything will work out perfectly. We won’t be here very often, because we’ll always be away guesting for all the top companies, and I will work for the Royal Ballet and you can work for ABT, so we won’t see much of each other, but —”

Tristan stopped in the path and shoved his hands in his pockets. To Alexandra’s surprise he looked upset. “What’s wrong?”

"I don't think it's funny when you talk like that."

Alexandra stared at him, even more confused and getting mad about her confusion. "What do you mean? Talk like what?"

"Like — all the us getting married jokes and stuff."

"Why? It's just a joke. Obviously."

"I know. It just makes me upset, okay?" He kept his hands in his pockets and they carried on walking down the path.

Alexandra searched for the right words, but she didn't know what she had done wrong, and the more she thought about it, the more it seemed like Tristan was to blame. "Tris, you're being a butt. What's wrong?"

"It's just, okay, we make a good ballet partnership, well, now, right? But it's just weird to talk about us getting married and stuff. I know it's a joke, and I don't know why it feels weird now, but it does. So can you just stop it?"

"Uh, fine. Whatever. You could have just told me that instead of getting all upset."

"I did just tell you that."

"Whatever."

They walked in silence for a while, Alexandra waging a war within herself between curiosity and the need to make Tristan feel bad for being rude. Curiosity won. "Tristan, what happened?"

Tristan had been waiting for that question, and his thoughts flew out in a series of violently emotional scraps. "I told Julian I like him."

"Good? Bad?"

"Bad."

"Okay, sad."

"No! He's stupid. I met this guy. On the Internet."

"On the Internet? Tristan, wtf?"

"No, like, I know him sort of from before. But we didn't really — like, I still liked Julian, right? But, I don't know, I started following his blog, and then he added me on Facebook and we've been talking a lot and stuff. He's so smart, Lexi. The stuff he says, it's just really helping me right now."

"Wait, do I know this guy?"

"No." Tristan spoke far too fast, and a deep red blush rose from under his skin.

"Tristan Patel, tell me who it is! Right now!"

"No! You don't know him."

"I totally do, you are a horrible liar! Come onnn, Tris, I won't tell anyone, I swear." Tristan shook his head, and Alexandra sulked. "You suck."

They began to walk across the green grass of the park, cutting a wide swath around a group of young adults playing frisbee. Alexandra felt self-conscious in her knit pants, the skirt of her costume hanging over it, and her thick blue academy hoodie over top. The bus stop was empty, and Alexandra sat down on the bench, tucking her legs up, and sitting cross-legged. Tristan sat down next to her and pulled out his Thermos of green tea, using it to warm his hands. "Your parents still bugging you about stuff?" he asked.

"Yeah," Alexandra said grimacing. She'd gone to her family dentist and then he'd had a talk with her mom afterwards, saying that he had suspected that she was throwing up. *How was I supposed to know that dentists could tell that from your teeth?* She'd accidentally told Tristan that her parents were upset about something, and now he wouldn't let it go.

"So, what was it? What did the perfect Miss Alexandra Dunstan of the perfect homework and dedication to ballet do to piss her parents off?"

"Tristan! Stop it, okay?"

"No, seriously, tell me, I can't picture it. Wait, I know, you didn't do enough homework, that's it, right?"

"Tristan, I'm this close to slapping you."

The bus came, and they got on, making their way to the back. "You going home now?" Tristan asked, holding on to the bus bar, his slim body swaying back and forth with the movement of the vehicle.

"Yeah. I've got so much homework. I'm afraid that I'm going to be doing what Andrew did in his last year next year."

"Andrew Lui? San Francisco Ballet, Andrew? Why, what'd he do?"

"You don't remember? When he was in grade twelve. He'd come for one day, hand all of his homework in and get the homework he'd missed, then he couldn't show up for the next day because he'd have to finish the homework he got from the day before, and he just repeated that all year."

Tristan shrugged. "He graduated, it's all good."

"Yeah, but I'd like to graduate with an average a little better than his."

"Why? Even if you do go to university or something it won't be for, like, a long time."

Alexandra shrugged. "I don't know. It's like a comfort thing for me. Homework, it's this constant, and if I'm getting good grades it's like even if dance or something isn't going well, at least I have good grades and I can be happy about that, you know?"

"Not really," Tristan said. "But okay." The bus stopped downtown and they transferred, heading over to the North Shore.

"Are we friends?" Tristan asked suddenly.

Alexandra frowned at him, confused. "What is wrong with you, Tristan? Of course we are."

"Just checking." Tristan shrugged. "I don't know, sometimes I feel like we are so close and we talk so much, but I don't actually know anything about you. That's what I like about … that guy. We talk, and it's like we're having this really open, real conversation."

Alexandra raised her eyebrows. "Uh-huh. Tristan, I'm kind of worried about you. I mean, if you're just talking to him on the Internet —"

"I know him from real life, though! It's not like that."

"Soooo," said Alexandra, starting to smirk, "what exactly happened with Julian? Did you find out if he's gay or not yet?"

"I don't know!" Tristan exploded.

"What do you mean you don't know?"

"Like, okay, so this was after men's class, and we were walking to the bus stop, right?"

"Yeah. Wait, when was this?"

"Like, two weeks ago."

"Wow, rebound much."

"Shut up. Anyway, so we were walking, and I said, uh, I said —" Tristan stopped, suddenly awkward.

"Whaaat? C'mon, tell me. What? What? What?"

"Well, I was like, 'I don't know if you are gay, or straight, or whatever, but I like you, and I thought you should know that.'"

"And?"

"I don't know! He just ignored it, and started talking really fast about something else. I know he heard me. I don't know. He's stupid."

"What the — yeah, that's super weird. Julian's strange."

"Yeah. Whatever. I'm over it."

The bus pulled up to Alexandra's stop, and she stood up. "Bye, love you, see you tomorrow. Don't talk to Internet freaks."

Also in the Ballet School Confidential series by Charis Marsh

Love You, Hate You
978-1554889617
$12.99

Kaitlyn, Taylor, Alexandra, and Julian are all students at the Vancouver International Ballet Academy where ballet and drama dominate everyone's lives.

Kaitlyn was the star at her old school, but the competition at VIBA is fierce and her reputation as a prodigy is threatened. About to turn fifteen years old, Taylor is a bit of a scatterbrain. She's got a lot of potential, but the teachers are frustrated with her lack of confidence, and her troubles at school aren't helping. Alexandra has done everything right, and she's determined to become a dancer, but the teachers at VIBA seem to be against helping her. Julian, at fifteen, loves dance, so going to a professional ballet school seems fun — even if it does take over every aspect of his life.

It's only their first semester, but these four students will have to push themselves to their limits to make it through their first major performance, *The Nutcracker*, and continue on the path to becoming professional dancers.